YEAR OF THE GUN

The storm exploded out of the north like a vengeance and covered the land with its killing blanket of white snow—this was the great blizzard of 1886.

But if the land was the same, so now were the men. Suddenly the big were no better than the small, the strong no better than the weak.

Survival in Montana was reduced to its simplest terms—man against man, gun against gun.

Giff Cheshire was born in 1905 on a homestead in Cheshire, Oregon. The county was named for his grandfather who had crossed the plains in 1852 by wagon from Tennessee, and the homestead was the same one his grandfather had claimed upon his arrival. Cheshire's early life was colored by the atmosphere of the Old West which in the first decade of the century had not yet been modified by the automobile. He attended public schools in Junction City and, following high school, enlisted in the U.S. Marine Corps and saw duty in Central America. In 1929 he came to the Portland area in Oregon and from 1929 to 1943 worked for the U.S. Corps of Engineers. By 1944, after moving to Beaverton, Oregon, he found he could make a living writing Western and North-Western short fiction for the magazine market, and presently stories under the byline Giff Cheshire began appearing in *Lariat Story Magazine*, *Dime Western*, and *North-West Romances*. His short story *Strangers in the Evening* won the Zane Grey Award in 1949. Cheshire's Western fiction was characterized from the beginning by a wider historical panorama of the frontier than just cattle ranching and frequently the settings for his later novels are in his native Oregon. *Thunder on the Mountain* (1960) focuses on Chief Joseph and the Nez Perce War, while *Wenatchee Bend* (1966) and *A Mighty Big River* (1967) are among his best-known titles. However, his novels as Chad Merriman for Fawcett Gold Medal remain among his most popular works, notable for their complex characters, expert pacing, and authentic backgrounds. A first collection of Giff Cheshire's Western stories, *Renegade River*, was published in 1997 and edited by Bill Pronzini.

YEAR OF THE GUN

Giff Cheshire

GUNSMOKE

This hardback edition 2003
by Chivers Press
by arrangement with
Golden West Literary Agency

ISBN 0 7540 8206 7

British Library Cataloguing in Publication Data available.

Printed and bound in Great Britain by
BOOKCRAFT, Midsomer Norton, Somerset

CHAPTER ONE

HE LOOKED OUT toward the river, which lay softened by the smoke haze hanging everywhere over the prairie, and beyond it saw the benchland and its jagged breaks. Off there somewhere was Bitter Creek, a name that meant violence, and the target point of his thousand-mile drive from Texas. Stringing past the knob where he sat his horse were three thousand dry cows and steers that had been on the trail all summer. He had brought them where men said he couldn't, and he was ready to swim them across the Yellowstone and drive north in defiance of anybody and everything.

"Hey, Nick! You let Charlie put saltpeter in the coffee tonight, and I'll shoot off his old whiskers! He's so jealous of us young bucks he'd do it!"

The words floated up on the dusty air from Mel Kinder, the swing rider drifting past. Grinning, Nick Benteen made a motion of the hand that offered no real answer. The boys had town on their minds; had it bad, for the windows of Yellow Bluff had shattered the smoky light down there at the edge of the river as the herd wormed over the rise just behind.

They were dirty men, all but three out of Texas, all as shabby and tired of sowbelly and alkali as was Benteen. Pressures had built up too long inside them, and soon he would have to stir up those pressures, in hopes of forcing the hand of the man or men who he knew had been planted in his outfit to kill him.

He had been met at the Republican, south of the Union Pacific, by somebody obviously working for Con

Shannon, the man who figured he threw a long shadow in the country yet to be entered. Benteen had been warned to ship at Ogallala, not to push a step farther north. Shannon was an old and ugly story to Benteen, and even more so now that he had his sights on Benteen's oldest friend. Benteen had laughed at the Shannon gunhawk and trailed on, knowing all the time that this day of reckoning would come. And now it had.

Off in the distance the horse band, nearly sixty head, kicked up its own dust. The point riders began to bunch the steers where he had told them. Back in the drag Wad Dennis thumbed the neck of his horse and sent it pitching. Somebody let go a Comanche yell. The trail boss started his horse in a lazy walk down off the sage slope of the knob.

Light in the saddle and just over thirty, Benteen was thick in the shoulder flesh but worked lean in his hips and legs. His hair was shaggy, a dusty brown, and when angry his eyes seemed the yellow-amber color of a bobcat's. Unlike some men who stayed alive by the gun, he wore no gloves.

He noted the dull dryness of the earth and again looked at the thin blue overcast of smoke. Back in Dodge he had read a newspaper dispatch from Miles City saying there had been scarcely a time all summer when the crimson of distant fires had not been visible on some horizon. He had seen such fires. In a day's time they could destroy the range of a dozen cattle outfits, and their ravages had added even more tension to the crowded range he had to enter.

Yet what he had left behind in the south was more forbidding. The market was down and still falling. A year ago Cleveland had canceled the grazing leases in the Nations, putting two hundred thousand steers on the move to market or new range. The trail wasn't profitable any more because there was no place to deliver Texas steers—except by force, as he was delivering these.

The chuckwagon, which he had piloted himself, was camped where a shallow creek slid down between wide bluffs into the river close by the cow town. He could see the smoke of Charlie's cookfire twist up toward that of the coppery sky. He skirted the drag where it was being drifted into the spreading herd. He felt his shoulders grow wide and tight, stretching the yoke of his sweat-streaked, faded shirt.

Somewhere Charlie Flynn had got hold of a canvas fly, which was now on poles at the hind end of his wagon, shading his work space and cutting down the heat a trifle. The wrangler's horse was tied to a front wagon wheel. A quarter of fresh beef lay on Charlie's work table. He knew his business, this short man of monstrous belly, and like all good cooks was temperamental. Even the trail boss was careful not to raise dust too close to the wagon as he rode in.

The wrangler was the kid of the outfit, around twenty. He squatted in the tarp shade with a cup of coffee in his hand. There was sweat on his brown, boyish face, and a false look of worldly wisdom. In all the trail towns coming up, like Dodge and Ogallala, he had been eager to cut loose his wolf, and it was a very inexperienced wolf as yet, Benteen knew. Kit Beckner was off a farm in east Texas.

"Who's goin' to town tonight, Nick?" Kit asked.

"The ones," Benteen said briefly, "who'll stay outta jail."

"Which," Charlie said, grinning, "means nobody in this man's crew." He thought the trail boss was tweaking the kid, but Benteen was in dead earnest.

"Aw, hell—" Kit began.

Benteen's rough voice cut him off. "Tomorrow we swim the Yellowstone, the worst crossing yet. Afterward we move into country we've been told to stay out of. I'm not goin' to have a hung-over, pooped-out crew on my hands, Kit. Get that through your head."

"Look, Nick," said Charlie, enjoying what he thought

to be a ragging, "he's got women on his mind bad. How'd he know we're marchin' to war with these long-horns?"

Kit looked ready to start a small war immediately. Benteen paid him no further attention, swinging down and leaving the horse for the kid to take out to the remuda. Walking to the far side of the wagon, he filled a tin pan from the water keg and scrubbed his hands and face. He ran a palm over his wild-growing hair and wiped it across his stubbly beard. He saw Kit toss aside his cup in a gust of temper and knew the other men would be much harder to handle.

As they came in from the herd they eyed Benteen, expecting permission to visit the town but waiting for him to volunteer it. He didn't. Afterward, he watched what he had told Kit progress from man to man as they took plates and made the rounds of the skillets and dutch ovens. He wanted it that way.

A man who had not had a drink in six weeks was a thirsty man; a man who had not had a woman in that time could be as dangerous as a penned bull wild with the scent. This knowledge Benteen used now deliberately.

When he had finished his own meal, he spun a cigarette and held the flame of a match to it. The creases at the ends of his eyes deepened as smoke lazed up from his mouth. The teeth behind his parted lips were white and strong. For an instant the smoke scudded back into his wide nostrils, then he spoke to the men around him.

"You boys know what we face. A year ago a hundred thousand steers had to find room up here when the Indian leases were canceled. There's been fires burning grass all summer. There's been two dry summers so that what grass is left is poor, with water plenty short. There's been nesters layin' claim to land. And here we are with three thousand more steers, all throughs from Texas that'll be suspected of carryin' the fever. It adds up to this. I'll need every one of you in top ridin' shape tomorrow and every day afterward. That means no town tonight."

They already knew his attitude, but the curt words tightened the features of every man who heard them.

"Damn it, Nick," Mel Kinder exploded, "there's things we need! The seat of my britches is worn so thin I can set on a newspaper and read the headlines. I can put my socks on from either end."

"Me," Wad Dennis drawled in his loose-voiced way, "I'll be honest about what I need. I hear there's a woman they call Tiger Lily in that town with real stripes on her belly. Kit don't believe it and we got a little bet."

Benteen wasn't worried about Mel and Wad who had trailed with him for years. The silent ones bothered him, men who eyed him in belligerence but didn't say what was in their minds. Kit went out to bring up the night horses. The others fell into evening routine— all but three men.

Benteen watched their faces closely, waiting for the play. He had lost some men in Ogallala, temporary hands who had wanted to go back to Texas. These three strangers had been prompt to ask for jobs. He had been obliged to take them on, in spite of his suspicion of their quick availability and readiness, right after his brush with the man bringing Shannon's warning to him. Since he'd tried to smoke them out, and it looked like he had succeeded.

"Me," said Buck Potter, "I'm gonna get drunk and find me a woman. Tonight."

He was a tall, grimy man, and his close-set eyes challenged Benteen. He was supposed to have killed several men in Nebraska and got off each time on an excuse of self-defense. The fingers of Potter's nervous hand scratched along his leg, below the holster. Benteen watched them.

This was the chance Potter had waited for, and Benteen had given it to him ready-made. He meant to make the most of it, a fact self-evident on his surly face. His saddle mates edged off, trying not to be obvious, but getting spread out, ready to chip into the quarrel if Potter needed them.

"I'll figure your time, then," Benteen said to Potter. "You other two feel the same way?"

"Make sure you figure it all," rapped Potter.

Charlie, starting in on the pans, turned slowly at that suggestion of dishonesty. Up on the wagon and hunting his bed, Wad Dennis froze, then looked down. Over at the rope corral Mel Kinder began to swing his body.

Benteen's voice was tight and low as he said, "You scum, you're not pulling your cheap self-defense stunt on me. Go tell your boss it didn't work, or start the play yourself. I've known since Ogallala that's what you hired out for. Now, damn you, earn your money."

Potter's eyes widened as he realized he was the one who had been baited and forced into a showdown. Then anger seemed to leap into his face. His fingers jumped upward and were holding gun grips when Benteen drew and shot in a single, spontaneous motion.

Potter's weapon exploded, then dipped slackly and dropped from loosening fingers. It lay useless on the hot ground. The free hand moved up to clasp the shoulder of the gun arm as he staggered back on loosened knees. He nearly went down but managed to stand rocking, his face frozen in shock.

His saddle mates hadn't had time to get started, even if they'd had the courage. And there was always Benteen's gun, ready to cut them both in two.

"If you'd ever been south," Dennis called to Potter, "you'd never have braced this man. Not many there ever cared to and them that did never lived. Dunno why he didn't blow out your brains instead of wingin' you. He could of, easier."

"He's never been south of Ogallala," Benteen said. "He's from the Sage Creek country, and he's on Con Shannon's payroll. Get ridin', Potter, and tell Shannon to send a man next time. Ask him if he's forgot the lesson I taught him two years ago at Belle Fourche."

"You mean he works for *that* Shannon?" Wad asked. "The one that thought he could drop you till he nearly got a gun barrel rammed up his—?"

"I mean that Shannon. Cheat, range-hog and the hirer of murderers to do his killin'. Potter—get goin'."

The wounded gunman and his friends were soon on their way, the fight taken out of them—at least temporarily. Potter had trouble staying in the saddle, but there would be a doctor in Yellow Bluff. The road outfit offered him neither help nor sympathy.

"Now," Benteen told the others, "you can go to town except for the night guard. Get back in time to let them go in."

Within minutes, all but the cook and men whose turn it was to ride night herd were on horses and streaking for the river town themselves.

"They're a good bunch of boys," the cook commented as the last of them disappeared. "They'd have stayed in camp without a peep if you'd really wanted that."

"Which is why they got to go, Charlie."

"And it's because you feel that way about 'em that they'd of stayed here."

Waiting at the trail camp with Charlie Flynn, Benteen wondered why his friend Einer Dalquist had not shown up. He had written Dalquist from Texas just before hitting the trail north, saying he would be on the Yellowstone at this spot on this date. A lot of trailing had gone into making and keeping that schedule. And a lot of sweat and pride had gone into bringing the herd of Texas longhorns to the northern plains.

There was a debt of honor involved, as Benteen saw it. Einer's herd had been whittled so far down that without new cattle he could no longer claim, under Montana law, the range that Con Shannon was already trying to take over. These were the needed cattle, and Benteen had decided to throw them into the fight, backed by his guns and his Texas men. Shannon would fight to stop these cattle every mile from here to Einer

Dalquist's Bar D range because of their threat to his plans.

When Benteen's debt was incurred, Einer hadn't been a Montana rancher but a trail hand with the outfit in which Benteen had broken in. There had been trouble, that first trip, with renegades on the border of Kansas. It had been a night attack, fast and savage. The night guards had been shot out of their saddles, the others shot up in their sleep at camp.

Benteen had been the kid wrangler of that outfit, out with the cavvy because it was Comanche country where horses could melt away like snowflakes. He had never known what swept him out of the saddle, had no memory except of coming to on the prairie, early sun bright on his face, a bullet through his chest. Somehow he had made the discovery that herd, horses and crew were gone.

His fear, he recalled now, was that he would not die quickly of his wound, that he would live to be found by the Comanches and die their kind of death. And that would have happened except for Einer, who went to look for the kid wrangler instead of clearing out with the other survivors of the raid. Dalquist risked the same death by torture in finding Benteen, taking him to a place of safety and nursing him back to life. A debt like that could never actually be paid.

Middle-aged even then, Einer had quit the trail. He had a motherless young daughter, and he went north to start a ranch in Montana. Benteen had stayed with the trail—booming then—graduating from wrangler to rider, then finally to an independent driver. He had been a good one, and had made money. But from that moment of waking on the prairie, hurt and almost abandoned, he'd carried in him a burning coal of destructive fury.

He had learned the identity of the rustlers and, over the years, had come upon and killed every one of them —standing up, face to face. And he felt that same rage each time he came upon an exploiter of the great cattle ranges.

He had felt it more deeply than ever three months ago when he received the letter from Einer, which he knew by heart:

Dear Nick: Just thought I'd drop you a line and say howdy, Nick. Seen Tom Longwell last summer, and he told me you're headquartering at Fort Worth. How's it going with you, Nick? I hear there's no better market for your steers than for ours. Not so good here other ways either. Too crowded, Nick, and us little fellers is getting squeezed. Fellow name of Con Shannon is making the biggest play.

Maybe you remember him, Nick. The story got around up here how he tried to cheat you on a herd you delivered to him on the Belle Fourche a couple of years ago. I guess he'd like to tack your hide on the wall if he could, after the way you handled him.

That's sure what he's trying to do to us. He's homesteaded and built fences that cut us off from range we always used. We're going to need it bad next winter, poor as the grass looks now. It's sure been dry Nick. I reckon he aims to clean us all off the range, and he's got all the big outfits on the Sage backing him.

My stuff sure showed up short at calf roundup. Don't look like I can hold my whole Bar D range, and I wish I had the money to buy more steers. Way it stands, Nick, my range is between Shannon's and the other nesters. If I can't hold it, they'll go, too. Then there's my girl Linda. I'd sure hate to leave her broke if Shannon gets my hide nailed up there on his barn.

What I thought was maybe if things ain't so good with you, either, we might kind of throw in together. I still got the range for it, and I sure need more cattle. Just thought I'd mention it, but you're likely busy, and this would only be a hornets' nest, anyhow. Well, take care of yourself, Nick, and drop me a line if you get the time. Your old friend, E. Dalquist.

Einer would never have made that indirect plea for himself alone. Benteen knew how hard it had been to do it for the sake of his daughter and neighbors. Even then he had phrased it as an offer to throw in together, maybe hoping Benteen needed help Einer could give.

Even if he hadn't been at loose ends, wondering where to turn, Benteen would have responded at once. The fact that Con Shannon was at the root of Einer's troubles had something to do with it, too.

Cattle had been plentiful in Texas, and Benteen had quickly made up a herd. He had dropped a line to Einer saying three thousand steers were on the road and giving the date they would reach this Yellowstone point of rendezvous.

It had seemed likely that Einer would have met him by now, and as the evening shadows stretched longer he began to wonder if he would ever see Einer Dalquist again.

CHAPTER TWO

THE RIDER who came up the creek between the tawny, red bluffs at twilight made a slight figure in the saddle. Benteen knew before closeness confirmed it that the horse was ridden by a woman. He was seated at the fire, drinking Charlie's coal-black coffee, while the old cook went to bed on the far side of the chuckwagon.

Off to the west the herd had grown quiet. Day's dying brought up the prairie breeze and all the warm scents of the sage and cactus desert were carried by it to mix with the bright pungency of the sagebrush fire. The stirring air fluttered the leaves of the gnarled cottonwoods by the thin-running stream, and already he could see the far-off, winking lights of Yellow Bluff well beyond the nearing rider.

She came steadily but unhurried to the camp. A girl who was fair-haired, of Norwegian extraction, he guessed at once; and who reminded him strongly of someone he had known very well. Her cheeks showed deep tan, noticeable even in the dusk. He thought her eyes were blue but the shape of them held his interest. They were large, elongated—beautiful.

He climbed to his feet and pulled off his wreck of a hat. All at once he knew who she was, and her appearance here alone was the sudden point of an icicle in his heart.

He said, "You don't have to tell me. You're Linda—Einer's girl. Where's he?"

Quietly she said, "He's dead."

Benteen could do nothing but watch her, not really

surprised, yet stunned and deeply grieved in that part of him that held so much of affection and gratitude. Linda Dalquist swung easily from the saddle and dropped the reins. Her body was of the supple fullness of a healthy, a lively woman. She offered her hand.

"It's good to meet you, Nick Benteen. Dad thought so much of you. It would have been wonderful for him to see you again."

"Shannon?" he said at last.

"A killer of his. There's no doubt of it. It was one of those rim shots. Just a murdered man with no good evidence as to who fired the gun. It happened right after your letter came. That gave him hope. He was at least happy when he died."

Her voice was low-pitched, even husky, and he knew that in happier times it could be warm and winning.

"Like some coffee?" he asked gently.

"Thank you. I would."

She seated herself easily by the fire, in careless grace, and he knew she was entirely at home on the prairie. Her riding clothes were plain and threadbare but they were neat and fitted her precisely. That told him much. So many of the prairie women were beaten and destroyed by the drabness and austerity, the drying sun and coarsening winds and the eternal alkali.

She made him sharply mindful of his own rough, shaggy appearance. He put his coffee on the ground, and poured some for her, while his mind thawed and began to kindle in the same rage that came when he caught coyote scent. Shannon again—Shannon—

"Did you see the letter Einer wrote me?" he asked.

"No. But I came on yours after he died and I was looking over his papers. So I met you, myself."

She was studying him very closely as she sipped coffee, perhaps trying to fit him to the picture her father had given her of him, possibly finding her own judgment at variance.

"He told me," said Benteen, "that he needed steers to hold his range or he'd not only lose it—a bunch of other little outfits would be wiped out with him. He said somethin' about Shannon buildin' fences to keep the little fellows off grass they'll need next winter. Sort of offered me a partnership. Looked to me like he was up against the old freeze-out game, so I headed north with some steers to put on his range. But I don't really understand his—and your—and my problem." Even as he spoke the thing progressed from Einer to himself.

On the ground between them Linda used her finger to draw a diagonal line. "That's a belt of badlands called Buffalo Bluffs. It's part of the Sheep Mountains and the water divide between the Yellowstone down here and the Missouri up there." She completed her rough diagram. "There's plenty of water on the north side—Shannon's. It's much drier on ours—the south. Shannon's Slash S and its big neighbors used to use our side for winter range. The breaks for shelter and the prairie lakes, waterholes and run-off streams for water. The cattle could be moved back and forth through the gaps in the bluffs. In a good year the grass on both sides is fine. But there's more of it on Shannon's side, and lots more room. After the nesters came, they reversed the old practice and wintered on our side then summered on Shannon's. Naturally, he and his big neighbors want that stopped."

Benteen nodded thoughtfully. "So Shannon fenced the gaps to shut you off."

"He fenced all but the main gap. Bar D—that's our ranch—sets there on land my father had the foresight to homestead. Our neighbors couldn't tie up the other gaps because they're too dry for a ranch headquarters. So Shannon had them homesteaded for him to make his fences permanent."

"He figures," said Benteen, "that he can starve out the other nesters. But Bar D has to be destroyed and taken over before that gap can be closed, too."

Linda agreed. "Our section's called Bitter Creek, and our gap runs between it and Sage Creek, where Slash S operates. Shannon tolerated Dad at first because they couldn't do anything short of killing him, and they weren't ready to—then. He could run his cattle on both sides, and since they let him do it for a few years the law protects his range rights in Sage Basin, the same as on Bitter Creek. As long as he could keep using it. That's why he wrote you the letter."

"He must have told Shannon he'd done it," Benteen reflected, remembering Potter and the other Shannon man in Ogallala.

"He had to," she said somberly. "Shannon claimed Dad no longer had the steers to claim those rights since he'd shown such a low count at the calf roundup. So Dad said he had another herd coming from Texas. I'm afraid he bragged a little about you and the fact that you were the one coming with the cattle. Actually, it was signing his own death warrant. Shannon thought that with Dad gone, I'd scare out and you wouldn't want to buy into the trouble and risk losing the money you've got invested in the new cattle."

"He was wrong, wasn't he?"

"About me. And I hope about you. But you've got to understand what a mess it will be, Nick—Mr. Benteen."

"Nick," he said, "and not Uncle Nick, either."

She smiled. "The steers the nesters had north of the fences are trapped there now. The grass on our side won't carry what we've already got there through the winter. And there's more that will be sort of personal to you. Your reputation as a gunfighter is known up there. Shannon's hedged against your refusing to back out to protect your investment. He's hired a well-known gunfighter himself. A Dike Scarfield. Do you know him?"

Benteen's eyes narrowed. He shook his head. "Never seen him, but I've heard plenty. Shannon's already sent one gunslinger after me. Wonder why he didn't make it Scarfield?"

"Probably afraid you'd recognize him. Are we still going to be partners?"

Benteen simply held out his hand.

Linda rode out immediately, Benteen having agreed to pick her up the next day at a Yellow Bluff hotel. Afterward the trail driver sat by the dying fire. In the long view, the problem was simple. A bunch of nesters were being forced to get along with half the range they had to have. They couldn't do that for long, and once they were destroyed somebody else meant to have that range.

In the immediate, personal view, it meant that Benteen was going to see that the land stayed with the people it belonged to—including himself, and a dead friend named Einer Dalquist.

He got his blankets and went to bed. But he was still awake when the first riders returned from town. They came into the camp to get coffee before going out to relieve the night guard so it could taste the pleasures of Yellow Bluff.

Drowsily, he heard Kit Beckner call, "You awake, Nick? I won the bet with Wad. That Tiger Lily never had any stripes on her belly."

"So you looked?"

"And that ain't all I did."

Daylight seemed to come too soon. The men were all on hand, clear-eyed and ready for work even if a little worn. At breakfast Benteen called for attention.

"Last night," he said, "I learned more about what's ahead of us. It's a real dog eat dog fight up there, with the other side holding the cards. Einer Dalquist has been murdered, and probably by Dike Scarfield, who's gone to work for Shannon."

"Scarfield?" Dennis gasped. "That mad dog?"

"A man who makes Buck Potter look like he had nothin' but thumbs. Boys, I don't like to gamble too much with other men's lives. If anybody wants to turn back here, he can and no hard feelings."

Nobody spoke but Kit, who said, "If Shannon wants a fight, let's give him a good one."

Charlie Flynn grinned at him. "Real proud of yourself this mornin', ain't you?"

Kit grinned back. "Bet you wish—"

"He sure does," Dennis agreed. "Let Charlie get what you can just once and he'd beat you to town."

"Yeah," said Mel Kinder. "To get his picture tooken."

"If I was as foolish as you stud horses," Charlie yelled, "I could show up the lot of you!"

Benteen laughed with the rest. That was why he loved these men, who accepted the prospect of death and did it with laughter.

"String 'em out, boys," he said. "Let's roll 'em."

He watched them gather the cattle off the grass and throw them on the trail, grazing slowly toward the river. Then he rode ahead to find the crossing, which lay two miles below the town. To his surprise, as he covered the last distance, he saw through the rock and sage the shape of a waiting horseman.

The man was a stranger and rode a saddle with a centerfire cinch, which was rarely seen in Texas. He was young, with a hard handsomeness, and he let a rough gaze rake Benteen.

"You the man with that herd of throughs?" he asked.

"Could be," Benteen replied. "Why?"

The stranger nodded northward. "I'm stock inspector for the roundup district that starts on that other bank. I'm warnin' you, Texan. Cross that herd, and I'll hold it for quarantine. All winter, and that means a feed bill that'd bust you. We ain't takin' any chances on gettin' Texas fever on our side of the river. There's loadin' pens in Yellow Bluff, and you'll make money shippin' from there."

"I'll see your authority for that talk," rapped Benteen.

"I'm tellin' you, and that's all it takes."

"Got the men to make it enough?"

"They're waitin' across the river. Don't try to cross, Texan. That's all."

The man spurred his horse and rode upriver toward

the town. He planned, doubtless, to cross by way of
the ferry rather than to swim the treacherous looking
current. He was getting set because he probably knew
his warning would be ignored.

Benteen sat his horse for a while, not doubting that
trouble awaited him on the north bank of the river.
But trouble could move as easily as he could move the
herd, upstream or down, and the showdown might as
well be at this place. He rode back to meet the Bar
D's and told the point rider to turn them into the
water promptly as planned. He would be waiting on
the other side to show them where to emerge.

The cook wagon was heading for Yellow Bluff to
stock up, then use the ferry, and he passed it on his own
way to town. He found the place to be another cow
town; a wide street laid out for turning freight wagons,
long stretches of single-story falsefronts between a few
taller buildings, rails, stockyards and depot of the
Northern Pacific, which had come up the river a few
years before.

Linda was waiting on the porch of the Empress Hotel, and her saddle horse was ready at the hitch rack
beyond the sidewalk. She rose to her feet and hurried
down the steps.

She read the darkness of his features and said quickly,
"Is something wrong?"

"No more than expected," he told her. "Just sooner.
There's a fake stock inspector layin' for us across the
river with a crew of tough hands. Ten to one it's a
Slash S outfit. We can't dodge it, so we've got to beat it."

"How?"

"I sure dunno, right now."

Her mouth made a small, despairing twist. "Bad
time to tell you this, but I've got to. A man I know
came to see me last night after I got back to town. He
thought we should know we'll be met at the next county
line by the sheriff. He'll have an injunction against
you bringing Texas throughs into the county."

"How far's the line?"

"Probably half a day's drive from here."

Frowning thoughtfully, he said, "The cook wagon's comin' in to stock up. I told Charlie to pick up your stuff. You stay with him."

Her eyes flashed. "Nothing stirring. I won't let you and your men take risks too great for me. If you're going to be that way about it, it's no partnership and the deal's off." She was already swinging onto her horse. He saw there was a carbine in the saddle boot. She looked like she would use it if pressed.

The ferry was waiting on the near bank, and the man threatening quarantine had apparently crossed over on the previous trip. The settler operating the flat-decked boat was whiskered and wore a cap so big it settled down on his ears.

"Fella that went over a while ago," Benteen said, as he paid the toll, "you know him?"

"Scarfield? Who don't?"

So that was Dike Scarfield. Benteen had a faint, greasy sensation in the pit of his stomach for a moment. Yet he knew Linda was still not to be turned back. The ferryman spat overside and busied himself with the controls. They began to float across the clear water with its yellow bottom, the cable trolley squealing. The river soon looked larger, meaner. The problem of swimming the cattle was big enough.

CHAPTER THREE

His MIND WAS BUSY with the situation as the ferry docked at the far float. Seeming to expect him to try again to send her back, Linda put her horse hurriedly up the bank. At his lead, they lost themselves in the river growth immediately, riding northeast the way the river flowed.

They said no more until they had gone over a mile, where he stopped. He could see the dust of the herd on the far side of the valley, above the river trees, and he also could pick out the point where the cattle would have to enter the water.

"Since it turns out to be Scarfield," he said, "that quarantine threat was all bluff, and he knew it didn't stand a show to work. What'll happen is that he'll let us get part of the herd in the river, then he'll try to mill it. He's got his gunslingers in that brush down there, waitin' to cut loose at the right time."

"What are you going to do?" she asked urgently.

"Take the wheels off their wagon. But first I've got a chore for you. I want you to cut around them on the side away from the river, which they aren't watchin' right now. Go past them mebbe a quarter of a mile. Soon as the boys throw the first steers into the water, you show yourself and motion them toward you. They'll understand and follow through. If the Bar D's swim on a long angle downstream, they'll keep out of range of Scarfield's guns. I'll keep him and his bunch pinned down where they are."

Her face was pale. "Do you realize what a desperate character he is?"

Benteen smiled. "I can get a little desperate myself sometimes. Go on, now. Do what I said."

Without further comment, she swung her horse and rode off through the brush, cutting widely behind what he felt certain was Scarfield's position for an attack on the swimming herd. Swinging down, then, he left his horse. He kept to the river edge of the brush as he went on afoot. The point of the herd had not yet appeared through the trees on the far bank. He dismissed the cattle for the time being, concentrating all his energies and all his kindling fury on the action immediately confronting him. That was his pattern in such a moment; it had to be.

His hunch that they had not expected him to out-guess them and cross to this side ahead of the herd, was confirmed when he came upon their horses, three of them hidden in the brush. The animals did not wear the Slash S of the Shannon brand, but that was of little significance since Scarfield was undoubtedly working for the big outfits in this nasty effort.

Benteen angled deeper into the softwood timber, his plan now formed in his mind. Harassment from the rear would turn them around from the river, keep them tied up. If he could stay with it long enough for the men with the herd to get the swim started and for the point riders to come over to help him, they could quickly wind up the business.

He first caught sight of a spur giving off a glint of sunlight. The man wearing the boot to which it was attached lay sprawled behind a low slab-rock at the edge of the trees, peering across to the far bank of the river. The Bar D's had broken out of cover, Dennis and Kinder still on point, the first flankers having come up to help them.

If he could have placed the other two ambushers it would have given him a chance to throw down on them and stop the thing summarily. But to make any such move, as it was, would be to invite disaster from hidden quarters. Benteen figured to get the racket going while the herd was on the far side. If the steers exploded, the harm would be held to a minimum. If they held together and swam as he hoped, they would be out of bullet range.

He crept deeper into the shade of the trees and stopped at the first thick-trunked cottonwood he reached. Before he vanished behind it, he took a look and could still see the herd coming down toward the water. But now he had lost track of the one man he had spotted. Like a fire fanned by a hat, his anger mounted at this closeness to his enemies. He could feel it crowd his will and tingle in his arms and gather over the eyes that stared implacably forward. He pulled up his sixgun and sent a bullet cutting through the grass. A man yelled sharply, probably untouched but surprised and worried.

Across the river a rider straightened in the stirrups, craning his neck this way. Close ahead of Benteen a man yelled, "Dike! Some son of a bitch got in behind us!" A gun blasted angrily, but Benteen knew his position had not yet been discovered. He saw that Mel and Wad were going right ahead throwing the Bar D's into the river. The noise itself, as he had hoped, seemed too distant to spook the cattle, and no bullets were singing out over the water.

He let a few slash through the growth about him before he shot again, instantly whipping in behind the trunk of the tree. After that he couldn't follow what went on at the river. Yet he knew Scarfield wouldn't follow it either until he determined what was on his rear. Benteen cut over to another cottonwood and shot again, then moved and shot once more.

He kept working toward their horses, his shooting revealing that fact. It had the effect he wanted, for Scarfield didn't care to be caught afoot when the whole Texas crew got to this side. When Benteen was certain they had started moving over to where they could hold on to their mounts, he quit shooting and quickly slid off in the other direction. He stopped to reload his hot weapon then angled left and came between them and the river.

The swim was going, and he saw Linda moving openly along the near edge of the water, well down from him. She was waving her arms frantically, motioning the riders toward her. The flankers who had come forward were steadily shoving steers into the water. He saw a swimming horse ahead of the mass, a man being towed behind it. Somebody was angling the swimming leaders downstream toward Linda, understanding the situation and the tactics with which Benteen hoped to meet it. Then Scarfield's men began to throw lead into the river, realizing the herd was going to be kept out of range.

With a low, bitter curse, Benteen rushed toward them. He could hear the crack of a rifle that was putting its shots well out into the water, but not yet far enough to reach the lead cattle. Benteen came charging forward, utterly heedless of his own safety.

Scarfield and his men had swung into saddle, to gain elevation and yet be ready to pull out hastily at the last moment. Scarfield held the rifle, and he swung it to slam a shot at Benteen, who felt the bullet rip through the side of his shirt. He fired, but they still had the advantage in range. He dived in behind a pile of rock.

During the next ten breaths it seemed inevitable that the Bar D's would be lost in the Yellowstone. They were angling downstream as he had wanted, but the rifle was throwing its shots close enough to harry and frighten them. In that interval Benteen crawled steadily, hearing the rifle empty itself then quit shooting. Before it could be reloaded, he reached the brush. He rose in a crouch, breathing heavily. He wanted Scarfield.

At the west edge of the brush clump he saw that he had them in pistol range, but Scarfield was on the other side of the group. His brown, sweating mouth pulled straight, Benteen whipped a shot into their midst. A man threw up his arms, then grabbed the saddlehorn, swaying and panicked. The horse bolted, and that turned the tide. Scarfield yelled something, but his men were on their way. He followed. Benteen could have shot him then—in the back. He had never solved a problem that way.

He waited until certain they were not just pulling off for a new try. Then, when he turned to look again at the river, he saw that they figured they had accomplished their purpose. The lead steers had hauled around at the beelike bullets pocking the water ahead of them. The mill was getting bigger by the minute. He could see a rider—he thought it was Wad—struggling in the water and swinging his hat and yelling at the maddened cattle.

Benteen went lunging for the place where he had left his own horse. Swinging to leather, he dug spurs and cut a straight line for the river bank, across the shingle rock and through the growth. But before he had sent his mount crashing into the stream, he saw that the threatened mill had been averted.

The steers that had been trying to turn back or crawl on top of each other were again coming toward him. The thickened, struggling line began at once to thin out. They moved straight across now, making for the closest dry land. He pulled back as the first of them gained footing, bringing their streaming spines into view. Within minutes the point was on solid river bottom and, as they came on out, he headed them up the river, away from another possible trap.

The riders stayed out there in the water, for the nervousness had run like a current back along the line of cattle. The swing riders were in the water by then, closer to the other side. The longhorns swam in a steady, unbroken file.

He grew aware that Linda had ridden up to him when she spoke.

"No wonder you have a gun reputation! I bet they don't tell Con Shannon you ran them out of there singlehanded!"

He was in the aftermath of wrath, trying to get down from it. This was a needling feeling, much like that which came after a man had spent himself with a woman except that it was unpleasant.

"They didn't hanker to be around after the boys get over," he said. "And don't forget that sheriff ahead. He might not be as easy to handle."

The outfit was not up the bench, through the breaks and away from the Yellowstone until noon that day. Then again the longhorn herd was plodding northward, the cavvy and chuckwagon moving abreast for protection but well to the right to keep out of the choking dust. Linda was over there, riding along with Charlie, having been convinced that her presence with the herd in such hard going would cramp the men, forcing them to mind their language and actions to a point that would grow irritating.

That was an odd quirk in a puncher. There was nothing he feared more or worshiped more than a decent woman. Most of them would have given their lives for their trail boss; they already looked as if they would seek the opportunity to do so for Linda. But they didn't want her helping them punch their steers or making them swallow their cuss words or interfering with their rough and bawdy horse play.

So Linda rode on her pedestal of leather, with only Charlie and Kit for company.

North of the Yellowstone the country was desolate, dry and harried by a hot, dusty wind as it rose toward the water divide. It gave Benteen the impression of having been a beautiful region that, through some monstrous oversight of nature, had never been given the vital element of sufficient moisture.

The prairies were well covered with vegetation, the grass that had supported the last of the buffalo, but it was now scant and seared. Along weak washes, dry because of two rainless years, grew groves of cotton-wood, ash and elm. Again there would be nothing but empty, awesome plain, rolling bare and brown, and occasionally badlands would break upon the flatness.

Into such desolation the crowding had forced cattle-men to come. Over it they must now fight because of that same congestion. Through it men like Shannon would seek to make their own self-serving gains. Ben-teen rode in a mood darkened by his awareness of Shan-non, his growing knowledge. His hatred of such peo-ple had been born on a prairie like this long ago. It had made him an individual of two distinct and warring parts.

First and foremost he was a cattleman. He regarded the great sea of grass running from the Mississippi to the Pacific as one of the two legs on which the lusty young giant of the West could always stand. Grass and minerals—they made a simple economy that had pro-duced great wealth and could provide more if con-served and used judiciously.

It was not being so used, and for this reason there was an anger in Benteen that for ten years had flashed and roared in the thunder and lightning of his gun. This was the part he did not like; it was assuming com-mand of him now. He accepted the change quietly and finally and had no further quarrel with himself about it.

He had told Charlie to pull ahead and camp the wagon at three o'clock with the idea of pressing on again after a short rest in hope of arriving before dark at the county line where the sheriff was supposed to be waiting with an injunction. Around two, wagon and horse band drew on into the forward distance.

Since Linda knew this country and the waterings, he left that matter up to her and stayed with the herd. There was a chance that the warning about the sheriff had been meant to throw sand in his eyes, and he wasn't running any risk of a more determined gun attack on the cattle in this country that offered so many opportunities.

Two hours later, coming out from behind an obstruction at the head of the herd, he saw far forward a stand of trees and knew there was some kind of water up there. He signaled to the point riders and rode ahead. They would rest an hour or so, and probably there would be water for the wagon but none for the cattle. He didn't mind that. Dry steers weren't so anxious to stop and graze, and before long he might have to do some hurried traveling.

Charlie had camped the wagon at a waterhole in under the trees but hadn't troubled to put up his canvas shade for so short a stop. Linda watched Benteen swing out of the saddle with a look of wonder in her blue eyes. He knew it came from the black mood that probably showed on his dusty, whiskered features.

"Have you got a dollar?" he asked her.

She tried to penetrate the mask of his eyes, but he saw she couldn't do it. She decided he must be joking and said, "Poor as I am, I think I could raise that much. But what do you need money for out here?"

"I'm going to sell you the herd."

"Me? Why?"

He swung down and helped himself to some of Charlie's coffee, which the boys called "Taos lightning in mourning." He didn't answer until he had made and lighted a cigarette. As he spoke smoke curled lazily outward from his mouth and came between his eyes and her.

"There's no use tryin' to run around the sheriff if he's waitin' for us, and we got to assume he is. Shannon got that injunction issued, and it'll be against me bringin' the Texas throughs into the county because of the fever danger. You know about the fever?"

"I've heard of it, but I've never seen it."

"Texas critters are mainly immune to it," he said, "but they can carry it into herds that aren't. For some reason, freezin' weather kills off the danger—mebbe because it's ticks or somethin' that packs the disease. Nobody knows for sure. So a through herd, which is one that come up without winterin' somewhere on empty range—can be mighty dangerous. In that Shannon's got a real point, and it must of been easy for him to get an injunction against me comin' into his county. The idea is, it'll be against me doin' that—not you."

Charlie looked up from his work.

"They've got to enjoin the owner," Linda said, "not the steers. If I'm the owner, their injunction's no good. And by the time they can get a new one, we'll be home and there'd be no use in trying it again. That's a bargain, and I'll take it."

"Just a minute," Benteen said, grinning. "I expect to buy the steers back at the same price. I got to put up a herd against your range to make it equal."

"Which is an even better bargain for me," she said.

Benteen wrote out the bill of sale and had Charlie and Kit witness his signature. Linda fished into a saddle pocket for her purse, then handed him the silver dollar that temporarily bought the Bar D's. "I can't wait to see Jess Wilson's face," she said. "He's the sheriff."

"What kind of a man is he?"

"Knows which side his bread's buttered on. He wasn't able to dig up a clue as to who murdered my father. But he knows the law and, in his way, tries to enforce it. I think you've got him scotched."

"But not Shannon," Benteen warned. "That's a man who won't scotch easy."

"Sounds like you know him pretty well."

"I've known a thousand Shannons."

"And killed a few," Charlie added.

As the riders came in for the coffee and warmed-up beans Charlie had ready, Benteen explained the change in ownership of the Bar D's. "We're workin' for Miss Dalquist now, boys, in case you're asked. It's her herd and I'm just her trail boss."

After a little rest, the Bar D herd trailed on. From what Linda could tell of the immediate country, that would bring them to the county line before dark. The surroundings remained unchanged, bleak, burned and forbidding. Around seven Benteen rode out to where the wagon toiled patiently northward.

To Linda, who was poking along with Charlie but riding her horse, he said, "Might as well go see what your home county looks like."

She nodded. "I'm not feeling quite as smart as I did. I'm scared."

"Let me do the talkin' as much as possible."

"Gladly—for once."

They started forward at a trot. She was an excellent rider, forking the saddle as a range woman had to do to work cattle. Yet she did it without self-awareness, as natural a part of her horse as he was of his own. He wondered about his attitude toward her, since her father had been so close a friend for so long.

One thing was sure; that friendship didn't give him a paternal feeling toward Linda. Her physical appeal was tremendous, setting up nagging but pleasant little hungers along his nerves. He had known about Einer's having a daughter, yet his mind seemed to have arrested her growth at some permanent coltish stage in a formless obscurity. This woman was probably no more than five years younger than himself. It was a discovery he had not expected to make.

CHAPTER FOUR

AFTER ABOUT TWO HOURS OF RIDING, they moved up through a low pass and crossed a bare saddle between the chewed-out bluffs.

"Look," Linda said, pointing, "there's a camp down there. Jess Wilson must have brought along some deputies. Do you think they'll try to seize the herd?"

"The tip-off said it was an injunction against me bringing the throughs into the county," Benteen replied. "Which is about the only legal move I know of they could make."

His own secret worry increased when, coming down the long sage slope, he saw half a dozen horses on picket near the camp. "Slash S!" he said in sharp wonder, when he caught sight of a brand he could read. "Mebbe it isn't the sheriff, after all."

"If so," Linda said bleakly, "Shannon's backing him with a war party."

Benteen was uneasy about going on in with her, but she was an essential part of his move. They seemed to have surprised the men, who apparently were waiting here for a herd to appear over the rise. They shoved to their feet, hard-eyed men with guns on their hips, wariness in the stiff, truculent pull of their shoulders.

Sight of the man who stood on the left started the fury raging in Benteen. Con Shannon was as big as himself, built on the same wedgelike lines. His face was heavy boned, pugnacious, and impatience rode him— a man so used to having his way he had lost all regard for diverging viewpoints. Shannon's eyes burned hostility at Benteen, as if he didn't even see Linda.

"Still makin' snake tracks, are you, Shannon?" was Benteen's only greeting.

Shannon's hair was brick red, and he was probably not over five years older than Benteen. The redness of the kinky thatch now lay under the brown of his cheeks, too, and the muscles of his neck had swelled. He flung a sharp, commanding look at the one man with a star on his vest. Wilson had a humped nose, gray piercing eyes, and was neither a fool nor a coward, Benteen judged. Then Shannon looked finally at Linda.

"Who told you we were here?" he asked in a voice that was heavy, harsh.

"Maybe we smelled your coffee," Linda said sweetly. "Or what my neighbors call your skunk scent."

Shannon made a kind of growl as he threw the hard stare at Benteen. "Where's them Texas throughs you got comin'?"

"Me?" Benteen said. "Who told you I had any—Scarfield?" The hint of light in his eyes mocked the cowman.

The sheriff spoke in a voice that, by contrast to Shannon's, was very mild. "I reckon this is my job, Con, and you keep outta it. Stranger, I take it you're Nick Benteen, and I got an injunction against you bringin' Texas steers into this county till they've been through quarantine."

"I said I don't have any Texas cattle."

"Then who owns that herd that crossed the Yellowstone this morning?"

"Oh—that herd," Linda said brightly. "I do."

"Horsesweat," Shannon snorted. "Don't let them throw sand in your eyes, Jess. Serve that injunction."

"So you want proof," Linda said.

Reaching into the neck of her blouse, she drew forth the bill of sale, which she handed to the sheriff. Wilson read it, his frown deepening. He stared at it long enough to read it twice.

He looked up in bewilderment, then switched his gaze to Shannon. "He's sold her the herd, Con."

"The injunction's against him bringin' the herd into the county, damn it. It don't matter who owns it. Go on and serve the thing."

"I got to quit you, ma'am," Benteen said, touching his hat to Linda. "You and your boys'll have to take the steers across the line."

"If that's the way the man wants it," Linda said.

"Tear up that damned bill of sale!" Shannon barked at the sheriff.

"I wouldn't advise that," Benteen said.

"I wouldn't, either," Wilson added and sounded like he meant business. "You been foxed, Con. Linda Dalquist owns them steers, and if Benteen don't help her come into the county with 'em, we got nothin' to stop 'em with. Time you could enjoin the bunch of them, they'll be on Bitter Creek with the steers."

"I've got somethin' to stop 'em with!" Shannon spat. His men shifted their feet, more eager than uneasy.

"Don't make a bad matter worse, Con," Wilson snapped.

Shannon stared at the ground, then scowled up at Benteen.

"All right. We got a smart Texas gunslinger on our hands. A hell-on-wheels who's got brains runnin' out his ears. Which adds up to another goddam rustler to throw in with the lousy tribe we've already got on our range. We know how to handle rustlers up here, Texan. Rope—and we've got plenty of it."

"Rustlers?" Linda breathed. "This is something new, Shannon. I don't think you've ever called us *that* before."

"It'll be in the Miles City paper," Shannon said. "So you might as well hear it now. Your smart caper won't get you what you think. The whole bunch of you was outlawed by the stock association when it met there yesterday. For range violations and for rustlin'—and also for connivin' to bring a bunch of diseased Texas cattle up here. So go ahead. Take your herd to Bitter Creek. It won't stay there long, nor you, either."

"Through talkin'?" Benteen said, very soft of voice. "Then try listenin'. Two years ago you tried to cheat me at Belle Fourche and got your fingers stung. The man you sent to head me off at the Republican didn't get any place. Buck Potter didn't, Scarfield neither. I'm here. I'm goin' on to Bitter Creek with Miss Dalquist and her herd—but only as a saddle passenger till we're across the line. So the hell with you and your stock association and all your slimy maneuvers and windy threats."

"This ain't doin' any good, Con," Wilson said uneasily, "and I'm goin' home." He started off toward the picketed horses. He was the more reasonable man, trying to do his duty as he saw it.

It was different with Shannon's punchers. They had come to turn back the throughs; they were still poised on the verge of violence. At one word from him they would go into it, and they waited for that word hungrily.

Shannon seemed to want to give it, despite the sheriff's warning. But he said suddenly, "All right, boys, let's get outta here. We'll try rope, mebbe, next time."

At Benteen's nod, Linda swung her horse and rode out. He followed, keeping himself between her and the men behind. But the crisis was over for now. Wilson had been a stabilizing force, however reluctantly, and Shannon had seen the wisdom of biding his time.

"So now we're outlaws," Linda said when Benteen had ridden abreast on the other side of the rise. "Well, that's not much worse than being pariahs, I guess."

"I'm scared it *is* worse," Benteen reflected. "The outlawin' is only a maneuver for somethin' worse. Shannon's got the stock association backing him, with the county officials in sympathy. We better not take that talk about rope too light."

Two days later the Bar D's came down into the wide dry valley of nearly vanished Bitter Creek and were home. Benteen had by then had a close-up look at the country over which the fight was raging. Although it seemed only a flat, somewhat broken continuation of the prairie that wheeled south to the high plains of Texas, he knew that it lay exposed to the polar winds that roared down from the north in winter and to the rain-screen of the Rockies that added a sucking dryness to the summer heat.

Yet it was cattle range, and where cattle ran, men warred.

Riding ahead with Linda, the last day of the drive, he had learned more of the nester settlement on this side of the long, hazy rim-line of Buffalo Bluffs and its now fenced gaps.

"In one sense," she told Benteen, "the Sage Creek ranchers had an understandable resentment of Dad. They used to use this range over here, not really needing it but taking advantage of the fact that it was here. They had tolerated Dad because they had to, and they took the attitude that he double-crossed them by letting other nesters come in around him and cut up the range on this side so it wasn't much good to them. They didn't understand Einer Dalquist. He'd always been a little fellow, too, and he had a soft heart, besides."

"I know," said Benteen. "If he'd had anything else, I wouldn't be here. He risked dyin' the kind of death the Comanches put out to save my life."

"Why, I never knew that," Linda said. "Which shows you what kind of a man he was."

"I know what kind of man he was. That's why I'm here."

There were nine nester outfits south of the bluffs now, she explained, two directly below Bar D, the others strung out on either flank, all taking advantage of the prairie lakes and waterholes that in winter made Bitter Creek a substantial water source. They were a motley mixture, some young, some old, some capable and some otherwise.

"I'd like to know more about Bar D's grazing rights

on the Sage Creek side," he said. "What protects 'em?"

"It's a territorial law—what they call the principle of customary range. When Dad came here he had it published in the newspaper and brand book that he was running cattle of the Bar D brand on Bitter and Sage creeks. That made it his range as long as Bar D's kept using it. Everybody understood that, even Shannon. It wasn't nearly so crowded, then, and nobody protested—until lately."

"Doggoned if I can see how they can outlaw Bar D, then."

Linda's smile was bitter. "We're rustlers. Didn't you hear the man say so? Get enough other big ranchers to agree with him and we are, even if we've never looked at another man's slicks. From what Shannon said the other day, the whole stock association has agreed—so there."

"It'll take more than a resolution on their part, and they know it."

"Anybody can manufacture rustling evidence who wants to."

Benteen nodded in somber agreement. Actually, in this era of the cattle industry, a home range was only a matter of theory. Stock drifted, mixed and scattered, and nobody cared as long as the brands involved were entitled to a share of the general range. That was the reason for the huge, concerted roundups spring and fall.

It was the cause also for the legitimate fear of the Texas cattle. If they spread over the range before proved harmless they could, potentially, cause terrible damage. He had to think about the throughs, now, how to handle them, out of his genuine respect for that fear.

They talked on, Linda answering his questions and showing a remarkable grasp of the affairs of Bar D and Bitter Creek.

The Dalquist headquarters proved to be attractive and comfortable but, coming in upon them finally with

Linda, Benteen saw at a glance that they could never accommodate the new crew, which he hoped to keep on to the man. She and her father had done the work previously, hiring only seasonal help. He would have to put up more buildings, not only because they were needed but to show Shannon that, instead of being destroyed, Bar D intended to grow.

He planned to return to Yellow Bluff immediately and send through a draft for money he had on deposit in Fort Worth. They would have to freight out winter supplies, as well as lumber. With one thing and another, he could keep the men busy all year, even though there were more of them than was justified in winter for a ranch of this size. But he had to have them, his tested fighting force.

Linda swung out of the saddle, and Benteen let her go into the house by herself. Her father had been dead for nearly three months, yet the place showed care, and he knew how hard she must have worked to keep it up. Looking about, he located the water trough and well Bar D had to depend on when the creek went dry. The herd would have to be drifted through the Bar D gap to upper Sage Creek at once.

It would be a steady problem to keep the throughs from drifting deeply enough into Shannon's range to justify the reprisals he would surely make. He would have to be careful until freezing temperatures had removed the danger of their carrying the fever and spreading it locally. According to Linda, that kind of weather didn't usually appear until December or later, which was at least four months away.

He watered the horses, then unsaddled Linda's and turned it into an empty corral. He had told the men to hold the cattle south of headquarters until he had taken his own look at the country along the upper Sage. The steers would have to be moved there promptly, with most of the horse band, since they had not watered since that morning.

Before he was ready to start, Charlie pulled in with the chuckwagon. Benteen told him to camp it under the trees along the creek bed. Then he rode out, the lowering sun hot on his left side, to see how great was his problem.

The walls of the main gap stood nearly half a mile apart—yellow, sandy bluffs. Linda had told him that Bar D's homesteaded land ran through it, giving a perpetual protection against its being closed unless Bar D was destroyed. A well worn trail ran through here, made both by cattle and horses. There was no sense of rise and fall to show it was a water divide, and he soon came out into what seemed a continuation of the country behind.

He rode on for nearly two miles before he came to a creek that would be a stretch of the upper Sage. It was still well watered, and this more than anything impressed him with the fact that he was really on the more humid north side. Looking about, he saw a top-of-land running out from the bluffs on this side. He rode to it, dismounted, and climbed until he could get a panoramic view. For a long while he examined the brown monotony of prairie, always frowning, then he descended, swung back to leather and retraced his route through the gap.

Returned to Bar D headquarters, he saw that the riders had halted the herd farther south. He rode on until he came to Wad and Mel, who idly sat their saddles on point. Off to the east Kit had let the saddle band drift to a stop.

"You can go on through," Benteen told the pointers. "But we're goin' to have to close herd till they're settled, and ride line from then till it freezes hard."

"They're gonna stay dynamite, are they?" Wad asked.

"With a mighty short fuse. Linda says Shannon's headquarters are only a few miles on down the Sage. We've got to keep our critters well away from there, or we'll hand him the excuse he needs for a real rampage."

"Man hires out to punch steers, he can expect to punch steers," Mel said. "Let's take these devils to Sage Creek."

The Bar D's were soon moving again. Seeing that from his distance, Kit hazed the horses forward. That was a fine thing about his crew, Benteen reflected. He had only to give general orders and they were translated into instant and expert action. He knew without conceit that it took a good cowman to command that kind of discipline.

Linda didn't like the idea of the men eating from the chuckwagon when she had a good kitchen and knew what to do in it. But she quit arguing when Charlie, his pudgy fists on his fat hips, demanded to know if she was trying to cut his job out from under him. Remorseful, she ate supper at the wagon that night.

Afterward she and Benteen rode out, heading west into the brassy sun hanging low in the smoky haze. It was half below the horizon when they rode into the headquarters of Eph Fadiman, the nester who had been Einer's right-hand neighbor.

A family man, Fadiman stood in the yard, stocky, work-roughened and with a face that showed much recent worry. A woman had come to the doorway of the little shack to watch the riders come in. She was coarse featured and heavy framed, but Benteen saw at once the humor and amiability in her eyes. Three children hung about bashfully, two small girls and a boy around ten who looked like Fadiman and regarded the younger ones with disdain.

Linda swung down, Benteen following suit. Smiling at the collective Fadimans, she said, "This is Nick Benteen—Dad's old friend."

Fadiman offered a ready hand, and its grip was powerful. His wife nodded pleasantly and motioned Linda to come into the house with her for women's talk. Benteen caught Fadiman studying him, making his private judgment.

"We couldn't believe it," the nester said, "when Einer told us you were comin' with steers. It's the only way we'll ever hold our range, Benteen, and you're mighty welcome." He laughed, a little nervously. "Even if I am a little afraid of them throughs, myself."

"You've got every right to be," Benteen agreed. "But the boys took 'em on to Sage Creek. They'll ride herd till we get cold weather."

"They've produced plenty fever, already. In Shannon." Fadiman pulled out a pipe and knocked it against the heel of a worn boot. "But we might get cold weather sooner than usual. I know a old Blackfoot I see sometimes. He was tellin' me the other day there's a heap bad winter comin'."

"How does he know?"

"They've got all kinds of ideas. This old buck's is caterpillars. When they get a wide band early, it means a stinker of a winter, he says. And they've already got wide bands."

Benteen rolled a cigarette while Fadiman loaded his pipe. They lit up off the same match.

"I once heard of some settlers," Benteen said, "who got exercised because the Injuns figured there was a mean winter ahead. So they worked twice as hard gettin' set for it. Except one man. He went and asked a buck how they could tell. The redskin said the palefaces were puttin' up heap much wood. That meant bad winter sure."

"Just the same, they're pretty savvy. Got to be, the way they live."

"What you men figure on doin' about roundup?"

Fadiman scowled. "Figurin' don't seem to help a damned bit. I just dunno. The stock association had its meetin' in Miles City two-three days ago, gettin' organized. The way Shannon's been acting, I don't reckon we'll get notified to show up, this trip."

"Looks like I've got bad news for you. We had a

little brush with Shannon on the trail. He told me you've all been outlawed. Bar D, too."

"God!" Fadiman said with a groan. "That means we can't even send reps. We won't get back a goddam steer that's strayed off home range. Benteen, we've got to ship beef this fall or none of us can live through the winter."

"Then let's ship some beef."

Fadiman flung Benteen a sharp stare. "What do you mean?"

"We can have our own roundup."

The nester puffed hard on a pipe he had let go out. "A outlaw roundup? They'd never stand for it."

"They'd try not to stand for it. I hear there's nine of you nesters. I've got seven men just off the trail who are pretty tough. And myself. A few would have to stay here, but we could spare fourteen or fifteen men. It's our only chance."

"That's right." Fadiman fell silent with a jaw that was tightened hard. He was thinking it through for himself, and again he said, "It's mighty goddam right, Benteen. How about you and me goin' to see the other boys right now?"

"You see 'em, Eph. Then come over to Bar D in the mornin' and let me know. Bring whoever wants to come. Make it early as possible because I got to make a trip to town."

"Benteen," said Fadiman, offering his hand again, "I think Einer knew just what he was doin' when he wrote you about our troubles. You're what we need. Somebody with the get up and go to take the fight to 'em when necessary. We ain't had it since we lost Einer. But I'm thinkin' we'll get it again."

Riding home with Linda, Benteen was thoughtful. Finally he said, "Many of 'em got families?"

"All but Jim Damon, and he's going to marry the Yellow Bluff schoolteacher pretty soon."

"You let the one single man on Bitter Creek get away from you?"

Linda laughed. "I wasn't in the running. Besides, I'm not the only Bitter Creek girl who lost out. When the word gets around you brought in a whole crew of bachelors, you'll see."

CHAPTER FIVE

THE CREW, except for the men with the throughs, had just finished breakfast the next morning when Eph Fadiman rode in with two others. The arrival brought the punchers to their feet, all sweeping hands to their trail-battered hats. The man with Fadiman was young, stocky and fair-haired, with a pair of genial eyes.

But it was the girl who riveted attention. She was dark, bareheaded and obviously pleased by the stir she caused. All three swung out of saddle, and Benteen was as aware as his men of the long, slender thighs of the girl in her tight riding skirt. Kit's eyes were gleaming.

So she's the other one Damon passed up, Benteen thought. *And she's sure smelled my bachelor boys.*

Fadiman said, "This here's Cassie Glade, boys. She lives with her daddy on a little layout over west of here. The fella here's Jim Damon. They're the only ones could come over this morning. But the other nesters say they'll go in on anything we decide to do."

"Suicide," murmured Cassie, "being less unpleasant than the prospect of ruination."

Benteen took the hand she held out to him. Her eyes met his with a wise interest that puzzled him. She seemed so young.

"When I heard Linda had brought home some Texans," she added, "I had to come over and see you."

"Believe that yarn about the horns and tails?" he asked.

"I'd like to believe it."

Benteen found his hand in the strong grip of Jim

Damon and remembered that he was the nester who hoped to marry a school teacher. He knew from Jim's manner that Cassie had been in the running with him even less than had Linda. He was frowning at her provocativeness, not bothering to conceal his distaste. It was as if he didn't consider her very good advertising for the Bitter Creek settlement, even though Benteen knew his men figured otherwise.

Cassie said, "See you all later," and turned toward the house, apparently to visit with Linda. Benteen saw the eyes of his outfit follow her, watching the smooth flow of her thighs in the snug skirt as she moved away from them. She had made a terrific impact, was as aware of her primitive appeal as they.

"Well, do we start an outlaw roundup?" he asked the two nester men.

"If you're still in the notion, we do," Fadiman replied. "Although we still don't see how you figure we could cut it."

"Tell me how they usually work it."

While they crouched down with cigarettes, Fadiman drew a rough map on the dirt. "Everything north of Buffalo and the Sheep Mountains," he explained, "is Roundup Number Nine. South is Eight. Each one is usually divided into two sections. The easternmost start at Fort Buford and Fort Keogh and work upstream. The western sections start farther west, almost north and south of us. They're the only ones we care about, since they'll pick up all our stuff."

"And drop it quick," Jim Damon said sourly. "Or turn it over to some damned rustling outfit with their blessing."

"I'd be willin' to bet," Benteen said, "that Con Shannon runs the northwest wagon."

"He always does."

"Then I'm gonna take half our men and join him. I'd like to recommend a man of mine—Wad Dennis—to take the other half and join the southwest section's wagon."

Both nesters were staring at him, hard and disbelieving.

"You mean work right along with 'em?" Fadiman gasped.

"That's the only way we'd have a chance. And if you'll trust me and Wad, I think we can cut it. When would they start?"

"Another two-three days, the way it usually goes. They have their meetin' first and elect the roundup captains, and afterward everybody's got to get set and on hand at the starting points."

"We'll have to be ready by day after tomorrow, then."

"By God, if you're game to tackle it, we are," Fadiman said. Jim Damon nodded his agreement. Yet neither one looked confident.

Cassie remained in the house with Linda, but Fadiman and Damon rode off, seeming relieved not to have her company. Grinning, Benteen thought he knew why that was. Fadiman had a wife, Damon a sweetheart, and it was certain neither woman would cotton to their mixing with Cassie Glade.

He decided to leave Charlie, Kit and Chunk Cooper at Bar D to look after the throughs during the roundup. To Charlie he said, "I've got to make a trip to Yellow Bluff and back between now and day after tomorrow. I'll arrange credit at the biggest store there, and order our winter supplies. You start in tomorrow and bring it out."

Charlie nodded. He was watching Kit, who still stared toward the house into which Cassie had disappeared.

"Think mebbe she's got stripes on her belly?" Charlie asked.

Kit snorted and swung on his heel.

"When she spoke of ruination bein' unpleasant," drawled Mel, "she plumb amazed me. If it ain't happened to her already, she sure hopes it will."

Benteen was grinning as he walked toward the house. They had pegged Cassie swiftly, for they would never have spoken that way of a woman they considered respectable.

Linda and Cassie were in the ranch house kitchen over coffee cups. Benteen held his hat as he walked in, and he thought that Linda frowned a trifle at the way Cassie's face lighted up.

He said to Linda, "I'm headin' for town. There's some Fort Worth business I want to close out. Then I'll put in our winter order. Charlie's startin' in tomorrow to haul the stuff out. Anything I can do for you?"

"I was just there," Linda said. She sounded cool.

"Do you want company?" Cassie asked.

Benteen would have backed out fast, but he had already gone too far. Lamely, he said, "You're goin' to town?"

She laughed. "Only as far as Martha Smithwick's. It's only three or four miles." She smiled at Linda. "Why don't you come along, honey?"

"Too busy. You run along."

By the time Benteen had saddled his blaze-faced horse, Cassie was outdoors and waiting for him. He caught the reins of her mount, where she had left it, and led it to her. She got up lightly, and they started out.

They had gone about a mile before he asked, "You surely don't run a spread yourself."

She looked at him puzzledly. "Because I came with the men to the meeting? No, I've got a father. But he had a horse to hunt up this morning and couldn't come. Although I was curious about the famous Benteen, I had planned to go see Martha, this morning, anyway."

"The famous Benteen?"

"Dad says you're one of the fastest men with a gun in the West. It was a surprise to find you so handsome, too."

"Take it easy," he warned.

"Why? I'm not afraid of you—not half as afraid as you are of me."

He glanced at her quickly. "Because you've got the most deadly weapons."

"How exciting. Most deadly woman meets most deadly man. I wonder what happens next."

Benteen blew out his cheeks. He had figured she was about Kit's age but she had the savvy of a woman twice as old. He couldn't help wonder whether it came from experience or from a too lively, too daring imagination. He decided to give her something to work on.

"What I see happenin' is probably altogether different to what you do."

"You sure?"

"Let's find out."

He stopped his horse so abruptly she looked startled. Hers halted obediently, and she was only partly smiling when he looked up at her from the ground.

"Get down, Cassie," he said.

"Now, wait a minute—"

"That's what I thought. You want a man to chase you, but you don't figure to get caught. So let's quit it. I've got more serious business on my mind."

He saw a stain in her cheeks as she regarded him; he saw the shallow shortness of her breath. To his surprise she swung from saddle and came down to the ground. He could hear the sudden crash of blood in his ears as he thought, *Who called whose bluff?* Her eyes were on him, angry, exciting, taunting. He flung a quick look and saw that the ground swells had cut them from sight of Bar D.

"All right, Texan!" she breathed. "Now what?"

He caught her in his arms and knew that in a moment he would forget they were on the open prairie where somebody might come poking along. She met the fierce aggression of his embrace with a response as old as women.

He pushed her back. "Now, get back aboard that horse before I forget where we are."

With a small laugh, she footed a stirrup and went up.

She could afford laughter for she had done more to him than he probably had to her. His blood roared in his veins, and his flesh carried an electric charge of wanting. He had never allowed himself the liberties he did his men, his responsibilities forbidding. She had seeped into this tight repression and made it a torment.

The folly of his gust of recklessness grew plainer as they rode on. He caught himself eyeing the country, seeking a copse, a hollow, any retreat where he could press her daring to its ultimate extent. She seemed aware of this unwilling eagerness, to be enormously amused by it.

They came down into the ford of an ancient water course, and it was she who turned her horse upstream into the concealment of the brush and trees.

Benteen walked into the bank in Yellow Bluff around four o'clock. The place was busy, with townspeople lined up at the two windows. He had to take place behind a fat man with a stained butcher's apron and hard leather cuffs.

When finally he stepped up to the wicket, he found himself looking into the bored face of an elegant young man with sideburns and a waxed mustache.

"Want to send through a draft on the Drovers and Grazers in Fort Worth," Benteen said. "By telegraph."

The clerk slid a form out to him, dipped a pen and handed it over. He seemed to be trying to hold back a yawn while Benteen wrote. When he looked at the draft that was pushed back to him, he glanced up in weary irritation.

"This supposed to be five thousand?"

"It's right the way I wrote it," Benteen said. "Fifty thousand."

"Yes, *sir*."

"I want it deposited to my account here soon as it clears."

"We'll get right on it, Mr. Benteen," the clerk promised.

As he walked out, Benteen was grinning at the difference forty-five thousand dollars could make. He didn't
look like a man with that much money, had never tried
to. It was only working capital to him, slowly and pain-
fully accumulated through the years of dealing on the
cattle trails. He wanted it here now, that was all, to be
able to back any move he might care to make with the
necessary financing.

He transacted his other business speedily, and by
nightfall was on his way back to Bitter Creek.

CHAPTER SIX

THE SLASH S WAGON was at the mouth of Sage Creek in the early morning, the camp rousing and stirring for the first circle of the first day of roundup. The night-hawk was whooping the horses to camp out of the dawn's obscurity, the cook was busy at the tailgate of the wagon, while punchers sat cross-legged, stuffing themselves against a morning's long grind. They were mostly Sage Basiners except for reps from other areas. Even the stray men looked tense.

Someone was coming, a party of four men who appeared on the rise to the south.

"Con!" a man shouted. "Them's nesters, sure as you're a foot high! One's the same blaze horse that Texan rides—Benteen!"

Con Shannon stepped away from the wagon where he had been eating alone, using the tailgate for a table and getting in the cook's way, a cold, aloof man with no gift for comradeship and no respect for the provinces of others. His pale eyes squinted as he stared hard across the prairie. His blocky shoulders pulled up, his thatch seemed to turn a deeper red.

He stood at the end of the wagon tongue when Nick Benteen rode in. Two other Texans, Kinder and Burt Friday, flanked Benteen, while the nester Fadiman was just behind. The dusty brown faces of all of them were set, and they were all armed. The roundup crew had shoved to its feet but for some reason chose to move no closer.

"You got no damned business here, Benteen!" spat

Shannon. "You know that!"

"You mean that little matter of the stock association outlawin' us?" Benteen asked.

"That's a silly question. You've got no place in this roundup, and you ain't even goin' to rep."

"Can we just watch?" Benteen said.

He was laughing at Shannon, but not pleasantly. It worried Shannon and every other man looking on from his camp. These riders wouldn't have come so far through the small of the night for anything short of the quarrel they had every reason to want. Benteen was ready but pretty sure Shannon wouldn't start it—not yet.

There had already been the taint of murder in this range war in the case of Einer Dalquist. There would be more, but Shannon had to keep as good a face on his actions as he could manage in order to hold the support of the stock association. All he had a legal right to do now was deny the blackballed outfits a part in the official roundup, and until Benteen made a threatening move, Shannon could only stand on that authority.

Benteen had already identified the men who had been with Shannon at the county line and two more—the pair who had hired out to him with Potter in Ogallala. Shannon had not expected a move like this or he might have had Dike Scarfield along. He might send for the gunman now, except that Scarfield was of such unsavory reputation Shannon would want to keep him under wraps as much as possible.

Apparently the same thoughts were running in Shannon's mind as he said, "Get outta here, now, and don't give us trouble. I couldn't let you join up if I wanted. It was the association blackballed you, not me, and don't you forget it."

"Just want to see how you work cattle up here," Benteen said, and didn't budge.

Shannon seemed to decide that indifference was his best weapon at the moment, although Benteen knew he would hit quick and hard at the first opportunity. Shannon began to tick off the crew in four pairs, assigning them to their morning circles. The first he ordered into the long, wild arroyo of Dead Cow Canyon, the others into the low hills right and left of the main Sage valley. As the parties rode out, Benteen began to toll off his own men. One fell in after each of the departing groups, not joining them, just moving along at a distance behind. Benteen was the last to leave.

He had picked for himself Potter's two friends who, at Ogallala, had given him the names of Cornell and Frisbee. They pretended not to notice him, and he stayed well behind. Once when they let their horses slope out, he followed suit. When they slowed to a trot so did Benteen, keeping the same distance in their rear. He could see uneasiness begin to eat at their nerves. They remembered what had happened to Potter at the Yellowstone camp. Finally they stopped their horses and swung them about.

"What the hell is this, Benteen?" Cornell demanded.

"Just watchin'," said Benteen, "how you northerners work your cattle."

"Thinkin' about a couple of back shots when we get in the hills, mebbe?"

Benteen laughed. "Did I sneak up behind your friend Buck? Go on, boys, or you won't have your circle in on time."

They went on, keeping to the main valley for some two miles, then turning up an affluent that came out of the west. They followed this to the roughs at its upper end. They were then on what Benteen knew to be the rim of a big circle, with the wagon and holding ground near its center. From this rim the pairs would split, and eight spokes of a wheel would be established. Everything gatherable would be driven to the center, and the country covered left clean.

As a trail driver, this range art was fairly new to Benteen. Yet he thought that his own years of handling mass cattle had taught him more about them than Shannon or any of his riders knew.

Cornell and Frisbee separated, going off in opposite directions to either side of the shallow creek, thinking perhaps that they had thus posed a problem to the dogging Texan. Benteen rolled a smoke and stayed where he was. Through the hazy distance in either direction he could see the Slash S riders begin to flush cattle out of the brush and gullies and start them moving in toward the wagon. He let them work at it a while and was soon sure they were cutting back certain brands. He, Mel and Burt had memorized those brands; Fadiman already knew them.

When the Slash S riders had worked about a quarter of a mile down the creek, Benteen went to work. He had more riding to do than they since he had to cover both sides of the stream, but they had a lot more work. A range steer is strongly imitative; if it sees cattle moving in bunches it tries to join the march. Benteen had lost many hours cutting out unwanted stuff thus picked up on the trail.

The cut-backs left by Cornell and Frisbee were easy to start moving again; all they needed was a shove. There were few outlaw strays this far down the Sage, and Benteen started them fast enough so that they soon began to cut past Cornell and Frisbee and join the growing gather. He could see the two punchers speeding up their work, trying to throw back the outlaws but they couldn't keep up with it.

Neither of them cared to come back and dispute the matter with him, and he hoped his men on the other circles were making out as well. Here on this shallow fork of the Sage it had become impossible not to round up the outlaw brands. Mass magnetism was doing most of Benteen's work. He simply helped it along.

The valley was soon thick with floating dust, and he had to pull his neck piece up over his nose. He realized presently that the riders were no longer trying to throw the outlaws back, but they passed up all they could. These Benteen hazed out of the brush and little side canyons to become willing pilgrims. Around eleven they came back into the main valley, into which cattle were pouring from other directions. The vast bawling mass moved down the valley to the wagon.

The milling herd still raised so much dust the brands were not to be read. Benteen had pulled off to one side, and very soon he was joined by Mel Kinder, whose sweating face was black with dust but who was grinning.

"We sure rolled 'em a snowball, didn't we?" he greeted Benteen.

"The biggest hump's ahead," Benteen rejoined. "When they've finished their cutting."

Fadiman and Friday came in together. They had taken a lot of cursing, they reported, but nothing worse.

When the dust cleared, Benteen could see Shannon sitting his horse over at the edge of the herd. He was waving his arms, while the riders about him were shaking their heads, trying, Benteen knew, to explain how impossible it had been for them not to bring in the outlaws. Then Shannon swung his horse and was riding toward the four men watching.

"He's ringy, boys," Benteen warned, "and he's gonna say plenty. Don't let it rowel you into foolishness."

The whites of Shannon's eyes looked baleful in his dusty, whiskered features as he rode up and stopped his horse; coming close, he seemed to have the magnified face of a spider.

"Brains again!" he said savagely. "You got 'em in aces, Benteen! But your goddam outlaws stay with the throwbacks! You can't ace your way around that!"

"Go ahead and do your cuttin'," Benteen said. "We're just watchin'."

Shannon rode away. The dust was clearing off the cutting ground. Benteen saw that two men had been left to hold the herd. The others had moved in to the chuckwagon where they were washing up for the noon meal.

"We better get our own chuck," he said. "We earned it."

"Thank God it don't have to be over there," Mel said with a nod toward the wagon.

They rode south again, back over the rise from which they had appeared that morning. Benteen knew they were watched closely, wonderingly. Out of sight, they lifted the speed of their horses.

The camp they had set up the night before was at the bottom of the other side, in a growth of old trees. Jim Damon and a nester called Ad Meadows were there, guarding the camp and its equipment and the precious extra horses.

"It work?" Damon asked.

"So far," Benteen said. "You have any trouble?"

"They ain't found us yet."

A meal was ready, and they ate hurriedly. Afterward they exchanged their tired horses for fresh ones, and Benteen added Damon to the group he took back to the roundup, leaving Meadows to look out for the little cavvy and camp. They were back on the sidelines when the cutting work began, around one of a burning afternoon.

Men on cutting horses went seriously to work, the quarrel crowded out of their minds because this was important business. They worked into the herd and began to push out threes and fours and all the association strays—but they brought out no outlaw cattle. New herds under different brands began to grow on various points on the prairie, held there by riders. Calves missed in the spring roundup, meanwhile, were getting the hot iron treatment, the honed knife in the case of young males.

The blackballed ranchers stayed on the sidelines and only watched, a word that by then must have become a goad to Con Shannon.

It was around four o'clock when Benteen knew that the herd was trimmed as far as Shannon meant to go with it. He said, "All right, boys. Come on, and keep rubbin' your rabbit feet."

He rode in on the herd and came up to Shannon, who

eyed him in bitter suspicion.

"Through?" Benteen asked mildly.

"That's right. We're throwin' the rest back, Benteen, and don't try to stop us."

"If you're through—and you said you were—the official cuttin' is over. We're going to trim it a little more, Shannon, and we're going to kill any man that interferes."

Shannon's breath seemed to stop; his neck swelled and his cheeks grew darker. Riders right and left had grown wholly motionless on their horses. Shannon shuttled his glance to them, knew that not a one was ready at that moment to back him.

His temper checked somewhat, Shannon realized that he had no more legal right to throw back the nester cattle than Benteen had to take a full part in the roundup. The stuff had been labeled as strays and refusing to let the nesters take them over would look queer. The men had seen that before Shannon, who still found it hard to submit.

"Trim," he blazed, "and see how far it gets you!"

"Take over, boys," Benteen said quietly to his men.

They had worked so long with great numbers of cattle it was no trouble to move the shrunken herd a mile or more over the prairie. The cutting went just as swiftly, Benteen and Kinder working out the outlaw cattle. There were less than a hundred head to sift to the edge and move over to where Damon could hold them apart, this being the remotest part of the range being used by the outlaws.

By the time they had finished, the Slash S wagon had struck camp and was pulling south toward the next holding ground, the cavvy moving with it at a distance. A little later the beef herd was started. None of the riders cared to come close to the little blackballed outfit.

When Fadiman ran his eye over the throwbacks and declared himself satisfied with the trimming, the steers were hazed back toward the range that had already been worked.

"By dad, we got more than I figured to this far down," he said. "That shows why we had such a poor range count at calf roundup. The circle riders just didn't bring the stuff in. Boys, I reckon we own more steers than we thought."

"Which don't ease my mind much," Damon responded. "Where we gonna get the grass to put into 'em next winter? They won't all make beef."

"Let's worry about that," Benteen said, "after we get this job finished."

"That's kinda my system, too," Fadiman agreed. "One worry at a time can be too many."

They moved the small cut of outlaw strays over to their own camp. Benteen recommended that they remain there for the night instead of following the wagon to the new holding ground. They decided on watches, three pairs to take a third of the night each to hold the strays and horses and protect them from molestation.

Ad Meadows had supper ready by the time they were settled for the night: beans, bacon and coffee. The sun fell below the western prairie in a blaze of smoky brilliance. The breeze built up a little, still hot and scented by the stunted plants that filled the seeming emptiness.

It had gone pretty well, Benteen thought, but Shannon had had all day to think. Tomorrow would be different.

As if reading his mind, Mel said, "Wonder if he's gonna send for Dike Scarfield?"

Benteen shook his head without much emphasis. "Doubt it. Scarfield's their heavy artillery, and Con hasn't run through his own string of tricks yet. He didn't know till we took the throwbacks away from him just how we expect to gather our cattle."

"Some day it's gonna be you and Scarfield, though," Mel rejoined.

"Likely. But it'll be a day when Shannon's got all his chips in the pot. Meanwhile Scarfield's got his own work to do."

"And nobody seems to know just what that is," said Meadows.

"That's part of the idea," Benteen said. "He's like a killer animal. Nobody knows where he is or where he isn't, or where he'll strike next and when. Who he's really workin' for, even. That's all calculated to keep Shannon's enemies on edge. But now and then Scarfield's gonna strike, like he did with Einer Dalquist. Who's next? That's what we're all supposed to be wonderin' about instead of sleepin' at nights."

"Is he out of a rattlesnake by a coyote?" Damon wondered. "Or a coyote by a rattlesnake?"

"Don't grade him down," Benteen warned. "I know his kind pretty well. He'll stand up and fight. But he'd rather back shoot because killing's his trade and takin' all that risk just isn't good business."

"Who *is* he gonna get next?" Meadows asked.

"It won't matter much to them. The less logic there is to the way he strikes, the more every man on our side's gonna worry about is it him."

Benteen was on the new holding ground at dawn, the riders who had been with him the day before again accompanying him. Meadows and Damon were to break camp and move the cavvy and the little stray herd to a new camp some place forward during that day. Benteen had a strong feeling that this present stretch of daylight was going to show whether they could complete their work here.

Since he considered Cornell and Frisbee to be the most dangerous of the Slash S riders on hand, he intended to dog them again if Shannon didn't call for the showdown before then. But the roundup camp displayed an elaborate indifference to the four blackballed ranchers quietly watching them start the day's work. Shannon made the same assignments as before, the circle riders only entering new country, farther south.

Cornell and Frisbee again rode up the creek valley, this time going well up before they turned right into a wide, waterless coulee. They gave no sign that they knew Benteen was following and once stopped their horses while Cornell got down and emptied his bladder on the hot sandy earth. Then they went on, riding leisurely.

The coulee was grassed, and they began to pass cattle that they did not disturb as they pressed on. The depression seemed to run for miles, and Benteen was beginning to frown in puzzlement when, far forward, he detected the tawny blank wall of its end. The job for the morning promised to be easy, with no stream to straddle, and few side areas to search out for steers.

Then, as they rode on, he saw that the coulee simply split and ran north and south instead of west, forming a T whose stem they had been following. Without a word, the two Slash S punchers separated, one going either way.

For a long moment Benteen sat his motionless horse, pondering it. He could not tell from his position how far the side canyons ran. He could enter one or the other, or he could wait here until they had flushed the laterals, then ride them both himself. In following either one he could ride blind into a gun trap. In waiting at this point he was losing track of both Slash S men, which was equally dangerous.

Frisbee seemed to be the more passive of the pair, which might make him the more deadly. Benteen flipped a mental coin, then swung the other way, after Cornell.

He was charged with wariness as he rode slowly, watching the foreground. Cornell was still out of sight but the tracks of his horse showed him to be riding deeper. There were steers in here, apparently a bunch that went out to water and then came back out of habit. Benteen reminded himself that he could be worrying needlessly, yet the suspicion in his deeper nerves remained unchanged. He stopped his horse, listening with keen attention.

Some vague part of his brain must have caught it, for in a moment he had the bewildering certainty that a horse was running somewhere in the great distance, traveling fast. Understanding crashed out of the same submerged region of his mind.

Up on top. The team was getting back together again, and he wasn't supposed to know it.

CHAPTER SEVEN

BENTEEN STAYED WHERE HE WAS until the faint, stitching drum of hoofs had died out. It ended so abruptly that he knew the horse had stopped, and this gave him a vague idea of how far ahead of him Cornell and Frisbee were getting their waylay set up. It would have been easy to have pulled back and let them fry their brains out, up there on some hot rock.

He dismissed that promptly. This was Shannon's retaliation, his plan for removing the nesters' new leader and ending the roundup of the outlaws. It was make or break, now, and he had to show Shannon that neither purpose could be accomplished so easily.

Frisbee must have watched covertly until he saw the intended victim ride after Cornell. He had known a way to climb to the benchland above the coulee. He had been obliged to ride swiftly, but had kept at a distance where the sound would not have carried to Benteen except by his sixth sense.

The way to get them was to act so promptly they would be the ones thrown off stride.

There was no place in view where a horse could be got on top, but a man could climb it anywhere. Benteen rode to the sharp west talus, swung down and trailed reins. He checked the loads in his sixshooter, made sure the piece still slid easily out of leather. Then he began to dig the edges of his boots into the soft, loose earth of the talus.

He rose out upon a continuation of the great prairie.

For a few quick breaths he lay flat on the ground where he had crawled up over. He couldn't see a horse or human figure anywhere, only the sage and shimmering waves of heat. The safest way to go on, he knew, was to cut the sign of Frisbee's horse. Watching to his right with every step, he moved straight out. A little later he was staring down at the deep-toed prints of a swift moving mount. These he followed on.

He came first upon the horse where Frisbee had left it, down in the bottom of a ground hollow that ran right and left, breaking into the canyon somewhere past a screen of sage. He picked up Frisbee's boot tracks. The man had run in his eagerness to set up for the kill.

Benteen left the hollow, crossing on to the far side then turning toward the canyon, using all the cover he could find and going slowly, soundlessly. They were gambling everything on the natural supposition that he would be drawn deeper into the canyon and thus into their trap. They meant to make it sure-fire, two of them against his one gun, even if they did not succeed in cutting him in two with their opening shots.

The careful thinking he put into his approach paid off. He came in to the lip of the canyon at a point a hundred yards past the place where the ground depression met the rim. Thus he moved in on their unwatched side, where they lay on the bottom of the hollow, protected from the canyon yet in a position to riddle anybody passing below.

They would give up or they would still fight.

Benteen, his gun in hand, called quietly, "Gonna be a parade down there or somethin'?"

They rolled their heads toward him in pained shock. Both of them held revolvers and it was the more distant Frisbee who chose to crowd his luck. They had once before been sent home with their tails dragging, and Frisbee didn't care to have it happen again.

He flattened himself in disregard of the closer Cornell and shot across Cornell's body.

The bullet screamed so close to Benteen he had to drop flat, unable to drill a retaliatory shot into Cornell's exposed and helpless body. Thus, for a few seconds, he lost sight of them, the edge of the hollow cutting them off. He was not foolish enough to show his head where it had disappeared from their sight. He moved farther from the canyon, four or five feet. When he got his look into the depression again, they had gained cover in the sage.

The old rage churned in Benteen and his lips pinched grimly. He knew one thing above all else: he must not kill them. Con Shannon would like nothing better than to be able to bring a manslaughter charge, if not worse, against him and get him held indefinitely. If they realized that, the two men now aggressively stalking him did not propose to serve as the means for such a trap. Benteen could hear slow, careful but audible movement on the blind side of the crest.

Frisbee's callous use of Cornell to protect himself had thrown Benteen into a bad spot. They were too smart to break over the crest, just as he had been, and as he lost track of them the danger to himself multiplied. He reached out and broke off a dry branch of the stunted sage plant close to him. Its sound was audible, was followed instantly by the crash of a gun in the hollow.

The roar told him that one of them had pulled off to his right, and maybe both had. They were plenty jumpy. Benteen thought about their cold, calculating killer brains. There was only one thing their kind understood—the power of the gun.

They were weighing this thing, having a choice now of pulling out and again being beaten by the man they had been sent to kill. At that point in their thinking their killer vanity would begin to work. Alone, they knew neither one could beat him but together they had a good chance, and they would take it.

Benteen inched forward until he could again see into the hollow. Then he threw the sage branch he still carried, and as it hit the ground below a gun cracked out in the farther sage. He sent a bullet smashing into that clump, pulling back a distance and instantly springing to his feet.

He moved hastily in a looping curve to the west, slid down into the hollow and started back in toward the canyon. That time he prowled in upon them directly from behind, where they hunkered in adjoining clumps of sage, intently searching the top of the hollow where he had just been.

"Your mistake," he called, "is thinkin' you can pull out if the goin' gets too hot!"

They swung, firing. Benteen stood crouched, his body weaving back and forth as he fought to control the old, flaming fury. His handicap was that they were too far apart, and the slippery Frisbee had already thrown himself farther into the sage. Benteen fired less swiftly than they but with more precision. Cornell took a drunken step forward, swiveled and fell. A bullet out of the deeper sage burned a welt on Benteen's neck.

He had to run for it, cutting into the closest cover. Bullets trailed him and he wasn't sure how he managed to gain the sage. He plunged on, his remaining enemy lost him, not knowing when the thread of his life would snap. He had one chance now, which was to get far enough behind Frisbee to drive him into the open.

He halted, muffling his labored breath. He lifted a hand unconsciously to feel the bullet burn along his neck, aware of how close he had been to death, and still was unless he could again outwit Frisbee. He heard Cornell's muffled voice calling something, almost pleadingly, as if he feared he was being deserted. Frisbee made no reply.

After a moment Benteen prowled on, his straining eyes glued to the sage clumps ahead of him, watching for some slightest motion to help him. He saw nothing but pressed deeper into the rank sage, counting his steps, then cut back toward Cornell. Once he accidentally scraped up sound, but Frisbee had by then grown wary of diversions. There was no gunshot.

Benteen carefully broke his piece and replaced the empties. The heat in the thick sage had him sweating. Cornell called again, and Benteen moved in toward him. A shot ripped out ahead, and he felt it tear through his shirt at his side. Then he saw Frisbee, just as the man gained his first sight of him. The twinned blast of their shots was one slightly drawn-out sound.

Frisbee shrieked and jerked, his face going slack. The man sat down hard, a look of confusion on his sweating, twisted face. Benteen moved up cautiously, but neither man had any fight left. Cornell probably had a broken bone in the gun arm he now nursed, which had knocked him out of the fight. Frisbee kept a hand clapped to the meaty part of his shoulder.

"Get to your feet," Benteen ordered, "and I hope you're hurtin' like hell by the time we make our report to Shannon."

He made them walk, lurching, drunken men, until he had picked up both their horses. The point where Cornell had climbed to the top was deeper in the canyon and was easy to descend. He didn't let them climb into their saddles until they had reached his own patiently waiting horse. Presently he was riding down the hot canyon behind them.

The morning was hardly half gone when Benteen drove his prisoners the last distance to the Slash S wagon. Shannon was there with the punchers holding the beef cut, the cook and wrangler. They were all staring in hard wonder as Benteen came in.

"Couldn't lose, could you, Shannon?" Benteen rapped out. "If they'd killed me, there was two to swear I started the ruckus. If I'd killed them, you could have held me for the sheriff and had me outta your way a long while. It didn't work. I could have killed them, but here they are—a couple more for your hospital crew."

Shannon gave Cornell and Frisbee a poisonous look.

"And now," said Benteen, "are you going to use sense or do you want to run your whole outfit through the meat grinder?"

"He started it!" Cornell yelled.

Shannon looked at him coldly. "Shut your damn mouth."

Benteen had a glittering mirth in his eyes as he stared at the cowman. "Mebbe you're convinced now that we're going to stay on this roundup. My two Texans are handy with a gun themselves. I dunno about the nesters, except one thing. They're family men. If anything happens to one of them, Shannon, it's you I'm comin' after. Personal and pronto. Now let's get on with the roundup."

He read defeat in the cowman's eyes but a yielding that was very temporary.

"All right," Shannon said. "What kind of a deal are you after?"

"What I said. Let's get on with the roundup."

Shannon didn't start any more punchers on circle to take the wounded riders' place since it was so late in the morning. The cook attended to the wounds as best he could, then Shannon put the men on horses and sent them in to headquarters with a tongue lashing that Benteen could not hear.

At the end of that afternoon's cutting it became evident that Shannon had accepted the inevitable. The throwbacks were turned over without protest to be worked by the nesters. But none of the men from Bitter Creek grew confident because of that.

Eph Fadiman expressed the main reason afterward: "We're still a long ways from having our own herd on our side of the divide. Mebbe we'll get it all nice and gathered, then have it exploded to hell and gone for us."

"Depends," Benteen answered. "Shannon handicapped himself by dragging the whole stock association into it with him. Now he's got to remember that what he does will reflect on it. Mebbe cost him support."

"He'll think of somethin'."

"That I allow."

Day after day, thereafter, the roundup moved up the valley. Each gather brought in greater numbers of outlaw steers, until finally the nesters were holding nearly two thousand head. It was grueling, exhausting work, riding every circle, cutting every new gather, then spending a third of the time needed for sleep in guarding the outlaws. Maybe Shannon was hoping they could not stand the pace, but Benteen and his men never once slacked it.

The end was in sight for them a week later—or the big crisis. The roundup would go on, working west and east, but it was Fadiman's opinion that it would not find enough nester stock elsewhere to matter. "We better take what we got and call ourselves damned lucky."

Benteen was himself of the opinion that Shannon might try to scatter the outlaws the last thing, nullifying the whole matter for the nesters. He likewise agreed that it would be folly to crowd for the few steers that might be picked up outside of Sage Valley.

They were still camping apart from Slash S and its confederates, and one night with a day's work left in Sage Valley itself, Benteen made a suggestion.

"We might make a little additional sacrifice," he said to the men in the camp with him, "and call it money spent on insurance. Let's cut outta here tonight with the herd. If they're plannin' anything, it would probably be for tomorrow—the last day."

Damon pushed back his hat and scratched his head. "Damned if I don't agree. We already picked up more stuff than we expected."

Fadiman and Meadows nodded.

"You know the country, Eph," Benteen said. "Take over."

"Be dead easy," Fadiman said, "if they ain't watchin' for somethin' like that. Cut south to Buffalo Bluffs, then west to the Bar D gap and home."

"Home, by God!" Meadows breathed. "To be truthful, boys, I didn't ever expect to see it again!"

"Can we make it tonight?" Benteen asked.

"If we start right after dark," said Fadiman, "we could at least get to the gap. I'll go tell the boys on night herd to get set."

Meadows and Benteen began to pack the crude, simple camp on the horses that had carried it, as it would be a great help not to be encumbered by a wagon.

"Way you keep pullin' that man's nose," Meadows commented, "he's gonna turn Scarfield loose again."

"I'm not forgettin' Scarfield."

Within half an hour after full darkness, the outlaw herd was on the move. Again Benteen and his two Texans drew dividends from their long experience on the trail. Benteen and Kinder pointed the herd, with Fadiman and Damon on the flank, Friday and Meadows in the drag. They drove like they always did, unhurried but crowding for all possible progress.

The first hours were fraught with tension, there being a fair chance that the herd was being watched, but they made good time. Around two in the morning the dark, rough ridgeline of the bluffs could be seen through the starlight. Just at dawn the outlaws turned into the Bar D gap. The riders cut east immediately on the south side, then let the herd drift to a stop.

"I'd sure like to see my missus and the kids," said Fadiman, "but we better stick with this bunch and hold it till we see what's gonna happen."

"You boys can handle that," Benteen said. "I think I'll head on south."

"South?" Fadiman gasped.

"Not as far as Texas. I'm just wonderin' how Wad and his bunch made out with the other wagon."

"Yeah," Fadiman agreed. "You better. Think somebody ought to go with you?"

"He's either got on top of it by now or been licked."

Benteen changed to a fresh horse out of the saddle

band, then rode out. He passed Bar D headquarters well to the east and thought of Charlie and Kit and Chunk over there—and of Linda. It was going to be good seeing her again. He hoped she would be pleased for more reason than that his part of the outlaw round-up had been successful beyond their hopes when it started.

The morning sun swung up over the prairie, grew hot and brassy-brilliant. An hour afterward he saw a heavy dust on the southern horizon. He knew what it meant—a herd coming on—coming into Bitter Creek.

He went on at a gallop and not long afterward met Wad, riding ahead of the cattle. The puncher came on with a ripping Comanche yell. Their horses whirled up to each other; they clasped hands across the gap.

"I only had to pull my gun once!" Wad said. "How many men did you kill?"

Grinning, Benteen said, "Winged a couple. Did you do what we did—decide to give 'em the slip before they could stampede you?"

"That's what we done."

"You trained under a good man."

"You're joshin'," Wad said, "but I ain't. I sure as hell did."

Actually, Wad reported, his experience had been easier than Benteen's. The ranchers to the south bore the country's general hostility toward the Bitter Creek nesters, but they lacked Shannon's personal interest in the matter. They had protested but were not willing to fight when they realized that an outlaw roundup was going to be conducted right along with the official one.

"But it left them touchy," said Wad. "Wouldn't want to tromp on their toes again if I could avoid it."

"What's your count?"

"Little over eighteen hundred."

"Which," Benteen reflected, "about doubles the steer population on Bitter Creek. We've got grass for a while yet, but I wonder about the water."

"We'll have to ship plenty."

"All we can. And we might as well throw 'em together and start cuttin' out the beef."

CHAPTER EIGHT

THE MORNING HAD STARTED at Bar D headquarters when Benteen rode in. At the chuckwagon in the creek shade breakfast was over, and Charlie made a greeting motion with the fat hand he lifted out of the dishwater. At the corral Kit and Chunk were saddling horses. He rode over to them.

"How're the throughs?" he asked.

"Purty well settled," Chunk answered. "And I got a hell of a lot bigger question to ask you. Consider it asked."

"We had a roundup," said Benteen. "If anything, it come off too well. We got a mess of steers to cut and get to the railroad before the water goes and they've chewed up too much grass."

"Want us to stick with the throughs or help you cut?"

"We've got enough help. You boys keep ridin' line. Shannon's sore as a turpentined dog, and it's hard tellin' what he'll do next."

Benteen glanced toward the house, which showed no sign of life. He wondered if Linda was still abed, which didn't seem like that lively girl. He went back to the wagon and poured coffee.

"Want me to dish you up some grub?" asked Charlie.

"If you've got any left."

"There's a plenty." Charlie grinned at the two riders heading out toward the gap. "You're gonna have to steer that kid. He's sure pawin' the ground for the Glade heifer."

Benteen glanced at him sharply. "She been back here?"

"Once, but give Kit the hoity-toity. That only made him worse."

"Make your trip to town?"

Charlie nodded. "Stored the supplies in the barn."

"The next thing'll be lumber. We've got to have more buildings."

"I'm ready to start haulin' it when you give the word."

"We've got some steers to ship, first. Seen Linda this morning, or is she still in the hay?"

"She's up," Charlie said. "Seen her come out for a bucket of water just before you rode in."

Benteen frowned, wondering why she had not come out to learn what had happened on Sage Creek. He ate his breakfast, rolled a cigarette, then walked over to the house.

The back door was open, and she was in the kitchen, drinking coffee at a table that showed she had eaten her breakfast.

"Hello," she said.

"Damn me," said Benteen. "That is sure a joyous greeting."

"Had your breakfast?"

"All but my final cup of coffee." He took a cup from a hook, went to the stove and filled it, a deep, uneasy guilt beginning to worm in him. Cassie had been over, and what had that little chili pepper said to Linda? He sat down at the table with her and drew on his cigarette. "Your dad never really needed the Texas steers," he said.

That brought her out of her reserve. "Why not?"

"The Sage Basiners have been throwin' back nester stuff for a couple of years," he told her. "We picked up too many fours and fives for it to be any other way. The nesters couldn't ride all the circles, the way we did this trip. They weren't suspicious, because it stood to reason the Basiners would want to get as much stray stuff off their range as they could. Shannon started whittlin' on you people even earlier than you figured."

"Well, I'll be darned," Linda breathed, her coolness finally gone. "How did you ever manage to do it?"

He explained briefly, dispassionately, the way they had gone about the seemingly hopeless undertaking. He watched her face change, losing its stiffness, warming with her rich vitality and her appreciation of the triumph. That only made him the more positive that Cassie had dropped something to her, although he didn't believe any woman would allude to the explosion that had occurred in that dry wash brush.

He saw how any display of possessiveness by Cassie would look to Linda, coming so soon, and Linda the more attractive woman. It would be like a slap in the face with a pan of bread dough, showing him up for a sniffing, pawing male animal like Kit. If Linda knew about Cassie's own hungers—and he had known from the start that she did.

He was so straightforward by nature he wished he could admit what she was thinking and tell her how little it meant.

"Nick," she was saying, "I'm very grateful. No one else could have done that."

"I'm rewarded plenty," he said, "to have you smile at me again."

Her cheeks colored a little. "I didn't mean to be cool."

"Heck you didn't. Was it because I rode a piece with Cassie, that day?"

"Well—not that but what she said about it afterward."

He could feel his flesh prickling. "Like what?"

Linda only smiled distantly. "It doesn't matter. After all, we've only got a business partnership."

"All right. Then ride out and see the gather with me."

"Why—I'd like to."

He saddled her a horse, then they rode east. Wad Dennis had thrown the southern gather in with the one from the north. The pack camp had been set up, and the men were eating breakfast.

"One more," Benteen said in response to Fadiman's invitation, "and I'd split down the front. Ready to start cuttin' beef?"

"We sent for the nesters who stayed home," Fadiman said. "Bullnose Wells and Ira Glade, for instance, are kind of fussy. They'll want to count every head of their stuff we brought in."

"If they've got any objections to make after us rescuin' their stuff for 'em," Benteen exploded, "the devil with Wells and Glade!"

Linda smiled a little, and he wanted to dust the seat of Cassie's skirt.

An hour later four nesters Benteen had never seen before rode in: Ira Glade, Bullnose Wells, Jake Smithwick and Frank Hollister. The latter pair he liked at once. Glade was a tall, scrawny man of sour mien and Cassie certainly had not got her warmth from him. Wells was nondescript in every way except for the heavy, upturned nose that gave him his appellation.

They began cutting the outlaws brand by brand, and as the steers came out of the stirring, dust-raising herd the beef cut was started, with the throwbacks kept apart to be returned to their proper ranges. The nesters agreed with Benteen that the herd to be trailed to the railroad be as large as possible.

After watching for a while, Linda left, more than willing to let him be the managing partner of Bar D but apparently no more than that. He knew that she meant more to him than a ranch partner, than Einer's daughter—and he had let the urges Cassie knew so well how to arouse get him off on the wrong track already.

He scowled deeply when, a little after noon, he saw Cassie coming in. He pretended to be busy, although actually the work was going on smoothly without much help from him. She rode up to him quite as if there had been no other man present.

"Welcome home," she said. "And congratulations. I

saw Linda at the house, and she told me how you ran Shannon up a tree."

"Tree, nothin'!" he said and wished he dared to ignore the long-fingered brown hand she held toward him. "It's pretty dusty here, Cassie."

"I don't mind."

Nobody seemed to be paying any attention to them. He looked at her more closely, realizing again how infernally attractive she was in the primitive way of the wanton. She liked sex, enjoyed using it in all its expressions and worse. She liked him better than he had supposed until this minute.

"Glad you're back," she said in a lower voice. "Be up to see me pretty soon?"

"Gonna be a busy little bee for a while, Cassie."

"Not that busy."

She had made up her mind to rope him out of the herd promptly, and he saw that a little late. He wanted to smash it here and now, but all at once knew that he had to go easy. All at once he saw the ultimate horror: *What if she claims I got her in trouble—or pretends I did?*

"Mebbe I didn't mean that busy, but there's somethin' I got to know. What did you tell Linda?"

Cassie smiled at him. "Not what happened. Just what will."

"Which is?"

"That when I dab a loop, no man can shake it—not even a Texan."

"And that didn't let the cat out of the bag!" he exploded.

"If she wanted to read something into that, is it my fault?" She reached out and patted his arm. "Don't worry, darling, you'll like it. How about tonight?"

He didn't answer as she swung her horse and rode out.

The crew worked straight through, and around five o'clock were finished with the job. Since he knew the nesters would not ask such a favor, after the work of the roundup, Benteen suggested that he and his regular trail outfit take the beef to Yellow Bluff. It would remain in danger until it was on the cars and ready to roll east to market.

Since they had not shared the hard, dangerous work of the roundup, Smithwick and Hollister offered to hold the beef cut overnight. The others, most of them worn to exhaustion, started home with their throwbacks. Fadiman lingered a moment, eyeing Benteen with a look of uncertainty on his heavy face.

"Dunno if this means anything," he said finally, "but I reckon I better tell you. Jake Smithwick's spread is over next to Ira Glade's. He told me somethin' on the q.t. this afternoon. Dike Scarfield's hangin' around Ira's. Now, wait a minute. I don't think Ira'd traffic with the enemy. It's more likely that Scarfield's just smellin' around Cassie."

Benteen wondered why Fadiman had chosen to tell him. Had it been to warn him how doubly dangerous Cassie could be?

All he did was shrug and say, "No harm in that Eph, if Glade and Cassie don't object."

"Ira object?" Fadiman snorted. "He's figured out already that Cassie can buy him protection from Scarfield."

Wad Dennis rode up, and as he arrived he pointed back over his shoulder with a stabbing, excited finger.

"Somebody comin'. And he's got somethin' on his shirt that flashes. Mebbe like a star."

"Goddlemighty," Fadiman gasped.

Benteen's jaw was bitten tight. A rider came around the upper end of the beef herd, and the lowering sun hit and struck back from something very shiny on his vest.

"It's sure enough Jess Wilson," Fadiman breathed.

Benteen agreed.

Wilson was alone and sober-visaged as he rode up to

them. He tipped a nod, saying nothing by way of extra greeting.

"Who you lookin' for, Jess?" Fadiman asked, unable to hold it back.

The sheriff scrubbed a hand over his mouth. "You boys'll do. I got a court order on me, issued yesterday. Placin' your steers in quarantine."

"Quarantine?" Fadiman said in a thin voice. "Which steers?"

"Every brand on Bitter Creek. Till after the first freeze."

"You can't do that!" Benteen said savagely. "Or they can't—Shannon—the stock association—whoever is behind it!"

"Take a look."

Wilson had extracted a folded paper from his pocket. It was very legal looking, very legal sounding as Benteen read it, and it verified what the sheriff had said. Every nester brand was listed, as was Bar D. None would leave their Bitter Creek range until freezing weather had removed the danger of disease.

"You can file a protest," Wilson said, and he sounded a little tired. "Make an appeal. But it wouldn't get you anywhere. They claim all your stuff's been exposed to Texas fever by the throughs you brought in, Benteen. Just remember you were plenty bullheaded about doin' that. And it looks like you ain't the only one able to think up a little legal caper."

"Whose work is it?" Benteen demanded. "Shannon's?"

"All I know is I got this from the district court to serve. I'll have to see it's carried out, Benteen. A platoon of Philadelphia lawyers couldn't get it set aside in time for you to make a beef shipment this year."

Benteen was slowly grasping the cold finality of that. The suspected throughs had crossed Bar D and gone on to Sage Creek's upper reaches. Every steer in the outlaw gather had been on range thus exposed. Shannon and his supporters would stick to the contention that all the cattle on Bitter Creek had thus been rendered dangerous.

Fadiman made a desperate motion toward the beef herd. "Jess, we can't winter them critters! We'd have been damned lucky to get through with the rest! We gotta ship!"

"That order says confined to Bitter Creek till after a freeze," Wilson said through tight lips.

"All right, Sheriff," Benteen said quietly. "We'll abide by it."

"That's more like it. Boys, I know you're up the crick, but I got no choice. Will you be responsible for it, Benteen, or do I have to ride around and serve this thing on all the others?"

"I'll be responsible."

"Good."

Wilson turned his horse and rode out.

"You said the right thing, Nick," Fadiman agreed. "Anything we tried to move off home range before a freeze would be grabbed and held from there on."

"That order expires with the first freeze, Eph."

"Which might not come for ages. Good Goddlemighty! Three months ago we were prayin' for more cattle!"

CHAPTER NINE

BENTEEN SAT DOWN at the kitchen table with Linda and Fadiman, who had accompanied him to Bar D headquarters. When she had examined the court order the sheriff had given him, Linda looked long at Benteen.

"That winds it up, doesn't it?" she said. "The county is handing Bitter Creek to Shannon on a silver platter. With a real low bow thrown in."

"We've got to take our lumps, Linda," Benteen said. "Shannon got rocked on his heels every time so far. I guess he's entitled to rake in a pot."

"Is that all you call it—a pot?"

"That's all it is."

"But what can we do?"

With a nod at Fadiman, Benteen said, "That's why I asked Eph to stop by. We've got to figure it out."

"That'll take a long pencil and a pile of paper," Fadiman said. His cheeks were wooden, his eyes withdrawn in bewildered shock, and he made a hopeless toss of his hands.

Benteen shook his head. "Mebbe only more plannin', Eph, and a lot of patience. I never told you, Linda, but I been figurin' on haulin' lumber out from town and puttin' up a bunkhouse and chuck-shack. Think we'll build a line camp on the upper Sage, too. With a lot of riding, we can hold the beef herd over there with the throughs."

"Wait a minute," said Fadiman. "I'm willin' to risk it, myself, but some will object to running the outlaw steers with the throughs. If the fever should break out—"

"Those that don't want to chance it," Benteen cut in, "will have to risk losin' all their cattle because of short grass next winter."

"Now, wait a minute," Fadiman retorted. "It's a mighty generous offer you're makin'. You'll graze off your range on the Sage if we take you up, and I don't know where that'll leave Bar D afterwards. But I'm thinkin' of characters like Glade and Wells. Ira particularly, since Bullnose just strings along with him. You give Ira the gift of a fine horse, and he'll complain because you didn't shoe it."

"Then let him look out for himself. You said you'd be willing to risk it. Did you mean it?"

"I did."

"Good," said Benteen. "I wish you'd see the rest of 'em, and let's leave it this way. Them that don't want to go along with it can cut out their stuff and do what they like." He looked at Linda. "Since you own a half interest in our Sage Creek range, it takes your permission, too."

"Anything you want to do is all right with me, Nick."

"Thanks."

"Well, I better get around some tonight," Fadiman said, rising. "Tomorrow we've got to do something with that road herd we made up so fancy."

After Fadiman had left, Benteen went to a pooled place on the creek, shaved, took a bath and put on clean clothes. Refreshed, he sat a long while on the bank, watching the night drift in over the prairie, and then the first stars come out. He was glad he had been able to conceal his own clawing fear.

He had made the offer of the upper Sage range, knowing he could stand a loss better than most of the nesters. But the fact remained that they now had half again the cattle the available grass could carry. Although winter would solve the water problem, that of graze would only worsen. If stock went into the bad months in poor

shape, as they were bound to do at best, the severe northern weather would be devastating.

They could still drive to the railroad at Yellow Bluff
after the first good freeze. But it would have been much
better if they had been able to trail out the next day as
first planned. By December the stuff would be shrunken
in weight, would bring a ruinous price in a market already down.

The fury was rising in him, the determination not to
be beaten by a man like Shannon. He had to find a
counter measure, and quickly. But he had no idea what
it could be.

The nesters began to arrive at Bar D at daylight the
next morning in response to Fadiman's message. The
first to appear were Ira Glade and Bullnose Wells.
There was nothing hangdog about Glade now. As he
rode up to where Benteen and his men were eating
breakfast, his face was red with anger.

"You sure raised hell with them Texas cattle of
your'n, Benteen!" he sneered. "You sure come to help
us, all right—right up the crick without a paddle!"

Benteen went on eating, not looking up. "I guess
Fadiman told you what you can do if you don't want to
string along with us."

"And that's just what we're gonna do. We come after
our steers."

Wad Dennis said, "Hell, you could let 'em eat a little
more Bar D grass first, Glade."

Glade gave him a withering look. "Mebbe you think
it's funny. Your stuff won't catch the fever. It's ours that
will. Except mine and Bullnose's. They ain't comin'
any closer to them throughs. They done enough damage—tied us up where we can't ship a damned head of
beef."

Others were coming in by then: Smithwick and Meadows, Hollister and Damon, and finally Fadiman. They
saw the belligerence in Glade, the uneasy sullenness in
Wells.

"They want to cut their stuff," Benteen said. "How about the rest of you?"

"We're stickin' with you, Benteen," Damon said. The others nodded.

"Who relieved you and Hollister on the herd?" Benteen asked Smithwick.

"Ed Brownlee and Pete Carell. They're backin' you, too."

"That's all the nesters, then, isn't it?"

"That's right."

"Your move," Benteen said to Glade.

Without answering, Glade and Wells rode off toward the holding ground under the long line of bluffs.

"Why the hell Bullnose sticks to Ira, I wouldn't know," Ad Meadows reflected. "Unless he's hopin' to get at Cassie. That wife of his'd point any man in some other direction, but he's sniffin' in the wrong pasture this time. Cassie wouldn't have him if he was the last man on earth."

"Unless he was the last man," Hollister corrected.

Benteen called for attention.

"Got a new idea last night," he said. "Thought of a rancher on the Little Missouri I used to deliver cattle to once in a while. He was tellin' me something interesting about the badlands there. Seems they're sure death traps for steers in summer because they're so dry. But it's just the opposite in winter. The wind's cut off, the grass stays pretty clear of snow, and the steers can lick enough snow to get along. Said stuff he's turned loose in there come through better than what he kept out."

"I've heard that, too," said Fadiman. "But it's a long reach from here to the Little Missouri."

"About a hundred miles. Three times the distance to Yellow Bluff and the railroad. Boys, I reckon I've asked you to take some big gambles, and you've seen one backfire bad. But I'm gonna suggest another. Don't plan on sellin' any beef on the December market. The price'll be down, the stuff'll be in poor shape, and mebbe there's no need for you to take such a loss. As soon as we're out of quarantine, let's move the beef herd and what other stuff the range here won't carry to the Little Missouri and turn 'em loose to winter there. We could ship from there as easy as from here."

"Meanwhile, what'll we live on?" Smithwick asked. "What steers we keep here?"

"I'll bank any man that needs it."

"You fixed to do it?" Damon asked.

"I'll do it."

"He's got the right idea," Fadiman said in mounting interest. "And if he can drive to the badlands in December, it's a chance to bring everything through the winter and sell it fat. But I got to ask a question, Nick. First you offer your grass, now money. Why should you do so much for us?"

Benteen made a disparaging motion. "Mebbe I'm not doin' it *for* you so much as doin' it *against* Shannon. He killed a friend of mine, Einer Dalquist, a man I owed my life. But that's beside the point, which is—do we make our plans on the idea of trailing to the badlands instead of the railroad?"

Every man there answered affirmatively.

Benteen was pleased by this confidence yet felt the weight of the responsibility. He had trailed many times in winter and knew it could be the toughest of jobs. He didn't want to think of the things that could bring havoc out of an apparently clear sky. Yet it was a chance for Bitter Creek to be stronger for the winter instead of weaker and to break even with the board afterward.

Wells and Glade were busy with their cutting when the others rode in to the holding ground. Their neighbors turned to with a will and made short work of it. The two soon had their little cut of cattle dusting over the prairie toward home.

"There, sure as hell, goes our two weak links," Jim

Damon said. "I don't trust either one."

"Whatever happened to Glade's wife?" Benteen asked.

"Died soon after they come here, maybe six-seven years ago. Worn out. Not from work—from Ira. But Cassie's different. She's like her mother but with enough of Ira's orneriness to tell him where to get off. She's wild, but sometimes I feel kind of sorry for her. She never had much love. Mebbe that's what makes her kind of man crazy."

Benteen was wondering about that, himself.

He let the nesters move the trimmed herd to the upper Sage. Returning to Bar D headquarters, he went immediately to the house to find Linda.

"Put a ribbon in your hair," he said, "and come to town with me."

She looked at him in surprise. "What on earth for?"

"They got a lawyer there?"

"A good one. Joe Enders. You thinking of appealing the quarantine order?"

"No," said Benteen. "I think we better draw up partnership papers."

Linda laughed. "Nonsense. Unless you don't trust me."

Benteen insisted. "It's hard tellin' what might happen to me, Linda. Even to you, the way things stand. We better not leave any loose ends."

"If you really want it that way," she said.

They reached Yellow Bluff around four on a hot and hazy afternoon. It had been a pleasant ride. An unexpected gaiety had risen in Linda, maybe because the badlands move had restored her hope, maybe for more cause than that. It occurred to him, once, that this was the first time they had been really alone, his men having been somewhere on hand since the day they met.

Joe Enders's law office was over the bank. Benteen told him what they wanted, the lawyer asked questions and agreed to have the papers ready for signing on the following morning.

Back on the street, Benteen said, "You better get a room at the Empress. I'll pick you up for supper." She nodded and moved down the street. Moving into the bank, Benteen learned that his draft had been cleared and the money was on deposit. From there he retraced his steps up the stairs to Enders's office. The lawyer looked up from his desk work in surprise.

"This part's private," Benteen said. "I want you to draw me up a will. The simpler the better. I just want it fixed so if anything happens to me my share of the ranch and a little money in the bank here go to her. I don't have any other heirs."

He attended to a lot of other business he had, got a haircut and shave. After supper, Linda said, "It's too hot to go back to my room. Let's take a walk."

That pleased him, and they headed down toward the river.

Coming to an inviting spot under the trees at the edge of the water, they stopped. Benteen leaned back on the earth, feeling the warm leaves and grass under his shoulders and back. She sat beside him, leaning on one arm, its elbow crooked backward the way a woman's did. She seemed serene yet very alive.

"I never knew much about your life," he said, "except that Einer had a half-grown girl somewhere."

"Well, my mother died when I was born, and I lived with an aunt. It wasn't an unhappy life at all, but it was better after Dad bought a ranch and settled down. He had a hard time doing it. He was a lot like you."

"You think I'll have a hard time settlin' down?"

"Not in Bitter Creek the way it is now. But I'm not sure about Bitter Creek if it's ever peaceful again."

"I'm not that hungry for—"

She put the tip of her finger on the end of his nose. "Now, now, Texan. I didn't mean to annoy you."

He caught the hand, and she let him hold it a moment, then withdrew it casually. Looking up at her, her eyes seemed almost taunting.

"Mebbe not easy to dab a loop on, after all?" he said, his voice very soft.

She gave a start. "What made you say that?"

"Just a old expression."

She came to her feet. "If you think I'm trying to dab a loop on anybody, you're crazy!"

He got up, brushing the leaf litter from his pants. "I don't think that."

"What made you say it, then?"

He wasn't going to tell her he knew precisely what Cassie had said to so offend her. But she was wondering about that silently as they walked back up the road, then followed the hot, glistening rails into town.

They were almost to the Empress when Linda called out suddenly, "Oh, Helen . . ."

A woman across the street was just about to turn the corner. She swung her head, smiled in quick recognition and waved a hand. She waited there until Benteen had crossed over with Linda.

"This is Helen Kinsey, Nick," Linda said. "Jim Damon's promised."

Benteen pulled off his hat as the girl held out her hand.

She was smiling pleasantly, a pretty girl with coppery hair curled into tiny ringlets at the face by the heat. "I saw Jim the other night," she said. "You have quite a reputation, Mr. Benteen."

"Don't mister him," Linda said. "He's hard enough to handle as it is."

"If you're who Jim's buildin' a house for," said Benteen, "I'm sorry I took him off on that roundup."

"The cattle come first," Helen said, laughing. "They always have in this country, and I guess they always will."

The girls talked a while, then Linda walked on toward the hotel with Benteen.

"When they gonna get married?" he asked.

"They hoped to this fall. But I don't know, now. No beef check, no wedding bells. That's another thing about this country."

CHAPTER TEN

BENTEEN WAS ON THE STREET early the next morning, before Linda had put in an appearance. Three beef herds, he discovered, were in from the official roundup, one holding north and the others south of the town. The sight of them was a taunting reminder to him of the way Bitter Creek had been treated. The herds also made him think of something else.

He had a lot of work to accomplish on Bar D before the onset of winter, with the range under present conditions threatening to require much of his men's time. But it was general practice for the big outfits to lay off a good half of their hands right after fall roundup was finished and the beef shipped.

He stepped into the Longhorn saloon, which was just opening for business. The bartender, busy washing something cut from sight by the mahogany top, looked up at him. "Mornin'. What'll it be?"

"Just wanted to leave word with you," Benteen said. "You'll be havin' a lot of loose cowhands hangin' around here now. If you want to do two-three a favor, pass the word that Bar D's hirin'. Winter's work, likely. Tell anybody interested to ride out and see me. The name's Benteen."

"I thought so," the bartender said. "But I heard you had a big Texas crew. What you gonna do with more men?"

"I got wood to put up yet. I want to do some buildin'. And range work's gonna be a little heavy. Mebbe you heard that, too."

"Yeah. And a sure way for me to get in Dutch is to help find you hands."

"Who needs to know, if you'd like to help a few cow-pokes find jobs? A lot of 'em will be willin' even if I'm supposed to be outlawed. They don't always cotton to being laid off to winter any way they can."

The man nodded. He was florid, and had the good-natured look of a convivial man. "That's a fact. Some of the boys get wrinkles in their bellies before spring comes around. I'll drop a tip or so, Benteen."

"Fine."

He went next to the mercantile where he ordered a wagonload of stock salt.

"What you gonna do with all that?" the storekeeper asked.

"Mebbe I'm gonna have to put a beef herd down in brine."

"So I heard."

"Might have to feed more men than I figured on. So when my cook shows up, let him have anything he wants. Since you likely heard also that I'm apt to go busted, I can leave some money on deposit with you."

"No need of that," the man said. "Just settle up the next trip in."

From there Benteen went to the depot, where he dispatched a wire to the man he knew in Medora. He left word with the telegrapher to send the reply out to Bar D when it came. Finally he climbed the stairs to Joe Enders's office.

The papers were ready, but Benteen only signed the will he had ordered, the lawyer and a man he called off the street witnessing the signature. Returning to the hotel, Benteen found Linda waiting in the lobby.

"Had your breakfast?" he asked.

"Not yet."

"Neither have I. Come on."

They ate in the dining-room again. She was graver this morning, and he wondered just how wise he had been in letting her know he understood why she was

so secretly offended. Come to think of it, it might have
sounded like bragging or that he took such matters too
lightly. But he wasn't going to bring the matter up
again in hopes of straightening it out.

They signed the partnership papers at the lawyer's
office and were ready to start home.

It was around noon when they crossed the river and
hit the Bitter Creek trail. Their horses were fresh and
they rode swiftly.

They were a few miles short of the dry wash where
he'd had his hour with Cassie when Linda said, "Let's
swing by Ad's place—Meadows, you know. He's got a
wonderful family. You ought to meet them."

"Like to," he said.

They cut an angle across the hot prairie, and a little
later topped over into one of the small, scant-watered
affluents of Bitter Creek. Benteen saw a duplicate of
Fadiman's place: a small, plain house, a barn and some
corrals standing stark and hot in the sun.

Meadows was away but his wife, to whom Benteen
found himself being introduced, proved to be a surprisingly tiny woman with only one leg, standing perched
on a crutch as she offered a thin rough hand. There
were half a dozen children, from a baby in a basket to
a girl around twelve.

"Have you had your dinner?" the woman asked
promptly.

"Late breakfast," Linda said, "and we'll be home
pretty soon. Thanks anyhow, Edith. Nick wanted to
meet you, that's all."

"Ad thinks a sight of you," Edith Meadows told Benteen. He shifted his weight uneasily. "We were about
ready to quit when you came to this country. We're sure
glad you did."

"You like what we're plannin'?" he asked.

She nodded her birdlike head. "I'd rather gamble on
a drive to the badlands than be cut to pieces a little at
a time."

"We see alike on that."

They were soon riding on, and presently Linda said, "Edith's an amazing woman. She lost her leg in childhood—some bone disease. They've had a hard time and the way babies keep coming—" She looked at Benteen, her cheeks coloring. "They're wonderful parents," she went on, "and as in love as two people ever were. She told me once that neither of them ever went with anybody else."

He saw how much importance she put in that overwhelming, pure kind of love, and it made him uneasy . . .

Back on the job at Bar D, Benteen threw himself into the work he had planned. The chuck box was taken off the wagon, and Charlie started for town, Wad and Kit accompanying him with two extra teams. They would pick up the new wagons and start hauling the lumber, salt and extra wintering supplies. He laid out the new buildings at headquarters, then rode over to the upper Sage.

Mel and Burt were there, that morning, keeping the throughs and outlaws thrown back from a line they had drawn for themselves above Con Shannon's holdings. Benteen looked over the range carefully. Finally, on the creek, he selected the site for a line camp. He returned to the south side of the bluffs and spent the rest of that day and then the next examining every foot of Bar D range. That gave him a comprehensive idea of the nester holdings, as well.

Late on his second day of riding he came home by way of Fadiman's place. The nester was there, and Benteen had supper with the family. Afterward, sitting in the front yard with Fadiman while they smoked, he began to talk.

"Eph, I had a hunch and it checks out. We all got a lot more grass than we figured."

"Where?"

"There are all kinds of back corners you people haven't ever used, including Einer."

"Sure," Fadiman agreed. "Either too far off or too

dry. You can't get a steer to graze very far from water unless you close-herd, day in and day out. That can't be done."

"There's another way. Salt."

"Come again?"

"I mean," said Benteen, "that we're gonna graze Bitter Creek and the upper Sage like they were never used before. There's a new day comin' to the cattle range, Eph. It's got to. People have to learn how to get the full use outta what they've got instead of fightin' for more."

"What's salt got to do with it?"

"Mebbe I can show you a trick. You put your salt in places the steers don't like. Only have to hold 'em there a couple of days. After that they'll go for water and come back to the salt. I've held herds that way when I got hung up where grass was short."

"Take a lot of salt here."

"I've got it comin' out from town."

Fadiman knocked out his pipe on his heel. "You're dead right again. I never seen that done but it ought to work. They want salt as bad as they do water. So you see they get settled where the salt is, and have to hustle the water. And you pick up a heap of grass you ain't been able to use before."

"It's what Bar D's gonna do, and I ordered salt enough for everybody."

"What they raise you Texans on? Fox milk?"

Benteen grinned. "Where's a good place to get firewood?"

"Gullyhead pine's all there is. You just go till you find it."

Returned to Bar D, Benteen discovered that the wagons, loaded with lumber, were back from town. Moreover, three men had come out with them, wanting work. They looked all right to him, punchers who worked with the big spreads but wouldn't be needed until time for spring roundup. He hired them.

He sent the wagons back to town the next morning. He turned the new men over to Chunk Cooper with instructions to find firewood and start getting it out. Mel Kinder and Harry Arno helping him, he started to work on the bunkhouse.

Things shaped up swiftly after that. The wagons finished their hauling. Benteen sent lumber to the upper Sage. He had the salt stored on the range, covered by tarpaulins, a little scattered on the spots he wanted the cattle to graze off first. He sent salt to the other nesters, then the wagons started bringing in firewood. After that, he was able to keep several men busy on the new buildings. They were roomy but crude, and went up fast.

A wire came from the Medora rancher. He had room to winter the herd Benteen proposed to bring him and more. He would buy it. Benteen's eyes gleamed. If he could get the cattle there, Bitter Creek could pull through.

By the first week of October Bar D was set for winter, or as nearly ready as brains and brawn could make it. But winter was not all they faced; Benteen kept remembering Shannon.

He gave thought to who he should put at the Sage Creek camp for the winter. It was a responsible job, one that could easily become critical, and he would never have thought of Kit Beckner had the boy not been worrying him.

On several occasions Kit had slipped away, and it was an open secret that he was riding over to Ira Glade's. Although he said nothing, Benteen didn't like it. It was probable that Dike Scarfield was hanging around there. Kit was wild, hotheaded enough to tangle with the man. And if that happened, Benteen knew Kit would never come out of it alive.

Sage Creek would be a lonely, isolated and time-consuming place. But the deciding factor with Benteen was the idea that it was also much farther removed from Glade's than was Bar D headquarters.

Kit reacted like a thwarted young bull when he got Benteen's orders, along with Cooper and Friday. "Any particular reason for you sendin' me over there?" he asked hotly.

"One," said Benteen, "is that you hired out to punch cattle. And I'm the man who tells you where to do it."

"It couldn't be you think I'm poachin'?"

"Kit," snapped Benteen, "I've never used a man for my private advantage yet. And that's all the backtalk I want from you. You can winter on Sage Creek or light your shuck for Texas and a mule and a plow."

Kit rode out with the other punchers but didn't like it, and Benteen realized that the maneuver would not keep him away from Cassie.

The next day on the range he got word of Ira Glade from Damon.

"Here's somethin' you ought to know," said Damon. "Ira's threatenin' to sell out to Shannon. Mebbe it's only sorehead talk, or mebbe he means it. If he sells, so'll Bullnose, and Shannon'll have a start on our side of the divide."

"He could mean it," Benteen said. "Shannon would jump at the chance, and it would be a way for Glade to save himself."

"At the expense of the rest of us," Damon said bitterly.

"I don't reckon he's ever worried much about the rest of you."

Benteen's concern grew greater as he finished his riding. He had never been on Glade's spread or seen Cassie since that day at the beef herd. He didn't want to see her now but he knew he had to talk to Glade and call his bluff. He swung his horse and rode west, the afternoon sun low in his eyes.

Glade's house sat beside some kind of little bottom-fed prairie lake, where grew a few straggling cotton-woods of great age. The house was small, standing close by the lake, and when Benteen rode in to it he found Cassie out in the yard showing an open surprise and pleasure.

"You sure took your time about coming," she said as he rode up to her.

"I've been rushed, and I come to see your father. Where is he?"

She made an indifferent motion. "Off somewhere is all I know. He never tells me anything. But he'll be back pretty soon. It's late enough so he must be getting hungry." She sounded bitter.

He swung out of the saddle, determined to wait for Glade but not liking the prospect of being alone with her. He didn't want to talk of the things she had on her mind, not now or ever. He trailed the reins of the blaze horse, then followed her up the steps to the shade of the porch. There was a swing seat there but she went on indoors ahead of him. Her dark, hoyden look, her slender, gliding body hit him harder than he had expected they would. Intimate memories rushed into his mind.

The minute he stepped in behind her she turned and came to him hungrily. It was awkward simply to step away, and he let his arms close about her and gave her the kiss she wanted.

"It's been a million years," she breathed against his mouth. "Nick, don't be like you are with me. I want you—"

·"Listen, Cassie—"

"I don't care. I knew the first time I saw you I'd found my man. I know I made you mad taunting Linda. I shouldn't have but I was jealous. I'm sorry."

She wasn't.

"You've got a different opinion of me than your dad's," he mused.

She stepped back, her eyes quickly angry. "Don't charge him up to me!" she said. "I'm not like him. I only live here because I haven't any place else to go."

He felt a sudden pity. Affection, the want of a man, someone beside Ira to take care of her—these things charged her and made her what she was. There was youth, health and glandular liveliness added to it. He knew as he had not before that she was a very unhappy girl.

"I don't blame you for Ira Glade," he said.

She came back to him. "Nick, please! He won't be back for a while yet. We can hear him coming if he does. Even if you don't like me any more. I just can't stand the way I feel."

It was hard to shake his head, to push her back. But it was no longer a matter of a hungry man availing himself of a hungry woman, no longer a fair trade.

"You think that it's just a man I've got to have, not really you," she said bitterly.

"All I know for sure is that what happened shouldn't have. And it mustn't again."

"Because of Linda?"

"Both of you."

"Because of Linda." That time it was not a question.

Patiently, he said, "There hasn't been anything but a business deal between me and Linda. Just the same, what we did was an affront to her. Except for that, there might be more than a partnership."

"You want more?"

"I've got to be honest," he said. "I do."

"I won't let her have you."

She lifted her head suddenly, listening. In the distance horse hoofs laid down their sound. Benteen slid to the door and saw two riders break over the slope at a good clip. "Oh, lordy," he heard Cassie breathe at his elbow.

As they came nearer he saw why she had made the exclamation. One was Glade—the other Scarfield. Benteen's lips pulled into a straight, hard line. This was the time. If he could settle it with Scarfield now, he would.

All at once Scarfield's horse pulled off. It whipped to the right, slanted back, then vanished over the top of the rise. Benteen swore softly.

"Scarfield, and he pulled off when he recognized my

blaze horse. Looks like you almost had more company."

She clutched the front of his shirt, looking up. "He comes here, and I can't stop him. But I've had nothing to do with him, Nick, haven't even encouraged him. You've got to believe me."

He didn't answer.

Ira Glade rode up to the house but kept saddle, looking suspiciously at Benteen.

"Nice company you keep," Benteen said.

"Scarfield? I just run into him. He comes here to see Cassie."

"That's a lie," Cassie said.

"Anyhow, what business is it of yours, Benteen?" Glade demanded. "She's a chippie, and every man in this county knows it. You can't blame 'em for comin' around all the time."

Cassie ran back into the house.

Benteen stepped farther onto the porch. "Scarfield's a killer workin' for Shannon. You know that. Moreover, I hear you been threatenin' to sell out to Shannon."

"What if I am?" Glade said. "It's my spread."

"And my business. If Shannon gets a toehold over here, he won't stop till he's got the whole of Bitter Creek. Apparently you don't give a damn about your neighbors, but I do. If you want to sell, I'll buy your place."

Glade only grinned at him. "I allowed you might get that notion, Benteen. But there's a little question of price. It happens I got hold of a purty valuable piece of sagebrush. I figure either side'd pay a real nice amount."

"You can't hold me up, damn you!"

"Con Shannon ain't a man to count pennies in this kind of ruckus."

Fury worked and ate in Benteen. All at once he saw Glade as something more than the weak-chinned ne'er-do-well he had seemed. The man knew the strategic importance to Shannon of gaining a foothold on this side of the divide. By playing both ends against the middle, he expected to make himself some money, at least to buy immunity from the damage the big outfits meant to inflict on Bitter Creek before the range war was finished. That made him a dangerous man, a role that seemed to please Glade enormously.

"I'm not goin' to be blackmailed, Ira," Benteen said quietly. "And before this thing's settled, you might be glad to get out with a whole hide."

"I played my own cards so far," Glade returned. "And I'll keep right on."

"I'll stop you from sellin' out your neighbors if I have to kill you, Glade."

"To hell with my neighbors. What'd they ever do for me?"

"You rotten—" Benteen said, and then cut himself short as he walked toward his horse. All at once he was aware of an embittered and dangerous enemy he had not counted on. And that, he now knew, had been a mistake.

CHAPTER ELEVEN

THE SALTING WORKED as Benteen had hoped. Sections of the upper Sage that had never carried cattle were now in use, and the same was true of the Bitter Creek side of the divide. It began to seem possible that the cattle could be carried through the winter without the long hard drive to the badlands. The nesters even talked of making a beef shipment from Yellow Bluffs. The steers in the outlaw herd still looked good.

The days cooled, the nights became crisp, and sometimes there was ice on the water buckets in the morning. By the first of November Benteen observed that the horses were getting their winter coats.

"Kinda early for that, isn't it?" he asked Fadiman, whose experience with the northern prairie was greater than his own.

"Sure is," the nester agreed. "Makes me think of that old buck and what he said about the wide bands on the caterpillars. Mebbe he was right. At least the hosses seem to think so. Well, we're a lot better set for a mean winter than we figured we'd be."

"If the range doesn't ice."

"That hadn't ought to happen for a long while yet."

But the clear, cooling Montana fall held on for the next two weeks. Then late one afternoon dark clouds rolled in on the horizon. Benteen hoped it meant rain, because water had become the main worry after the problem of grass had been solved.

He awakened in the new bunkhouse that night to hear the howl of wind.

He grew aware that the interior air was far colder than usual. His blankets didn't keep it all out. Somebody seemed to know of his stirring and whispered, "If it's whippin' us up a rain, I'll believe in God again." It was Wad Dennis speaking.

For some reason Benteen could not go back to sleep. The wind's low moan raised in pitch. Finally he got out of the bunk and padded to the door. It slapped hard against him when he loosened the latch.

"Wad!" he said, not aware that he yelled. "It's snowin'!"

The gritty particles of snow came in on a knifing wind; the cold swept through the room. But, because of the sudden pushing excitement in him, Benteen stepped out far enough to seize the bail of the water bucket on the bench at the outside wall. The bucket swung heavily in his hand. He stepped in and pushed the door closed, suddenly aware that he made a ridiculous figure in his snow-powdered underwear. But the bucket—frozen solid!

The quarantine was over.

Everybody in the bunkhouse was stirring by then and somebody dragged a match along the side of the table and lighted a lamp. Benteen stared at the ice in the bucket, solid and frosty as if it had been frozen so swiftly it had writhed in torment. Six weeks earlier than they had dared to expect it. How do you like that, Shannon? We can still ship beef!

The punchers all had to look at the bucket of solid ice. They passed it from hand to hand and grinned, standing cold in the interior air.

Wad said, "It weren't rain, but I believe in God again anyhow."

"Go back to bed, boys," Benteen said, still grinning. "Mebbe a real busy day's comin' tomorrow." He blew out the lamp himself.

He hadn't a wink of sleep left in him. The wind, at first a low, steady moan, had risen in pitch until at times it gave forth a gusty scream as it rent itself somewhere outdoors. Now he could hear the abrasive grind of the snow driven against the window above his bunk. Coming this early, so unpredictably unseasonal, the storm could not last long. A day or two, he thought hopefully, a freeze-up to end the quarantine, then good weather for trailing to the railroad.

The wind was soon a heavy, rumbling roar coming without letup across the prairie. It had all at once an ominous sound to Benteen. He was remembering the Indians' uneasiness, the wide bands on the caterpillars, the early winter coats the horses were growing. This might not be the wonderful break he had hoped. What if there was no moderation, no more good weather at all?

He scarcely dared to consider the consequences: a range glazed over with ice on which walking, hide-covered skeletons drifted on the destroying winds. Men fighting the drifts and dying in them or going mad from sheer despair. An end to the quarantine with the mocking irony that it was the end of everything else.

He dared not think further and lay with a puckering tightness in his stomach. Sometimes he could feel the bunkhouse tremble and shake, hear timbers snap and groan. The cold chewed through his blankets and into him. He grew drowsy and fell asleep with the howling a pain in his ears.

The fire had burned out, it was cold again and daylight when he awakened. But it was weak light, half destroyed by the continuing storm and the opaque ice shield on the windows. He got dressed, hurrying in the cold. He found the sheepskin coat he had bought in Yellow Bluff on Fadiman's recommendation, and he pulled his hat tight on his head before he stepped outside.

Wind pushed him over against the wall. Tugging the door shut behind him, he straightened and stared out across the ranch yard, all altered and strange from the snow. He could see the main house and its icy windows and thought of Linda there alone, wondering if she had been uneasy in the night's screaming wind. The cookshack and commissary, all one long building, was more clearly visible. He could just make out the barn.

Lurching into the wind he tramped across the blown, wavy snow—only three or four inches on the average—to Charlie's place of business. The door exploded inward as he lifted the latch, and he stepped into warm, interior air. Charlie was at the stove, a man who would let nothing prevent him from providing three hot meals a day on time.

"A stinkeroo," Charlie said.

"It's the freeze the court order mentioned. Tomorrow you can start your fire with that piece of paper. Lord, Charlie, is this a typical Montana winter?"

Charlie had already started to fry hot cakes for Benteen. He turned them over lovingly, reached a cup and filled it with coffee. Benteen accepted the steaming black brew and took a sip.

"If so," Charlie said finally, "I'm headin' south on the next flight of birds. If they ever can fly again."

"Then I hope it's mighty unusual."

"Hell, man, you know I wouldn't quit this outfit."

Linda came into the kitchen, and poured some coffee. She ate at the cook-house now, which was a great flattery to Charlie. "It's terrific, isn't it?"

"If it knocks off, we can ship beef."

"It's got to stop. At Christmas, maybe, we have snow. But never at Thanksgiving. Eaten?"

"Only a light breakfast. Two-three dozen of Charlie's flapjacks. But I got to go down to the corrals and see if the horses have got their legs sticking straight up. And I better go over to the Sage Creek camp. North wind. They're catchin' it worse over there."

"Don't try till it clears," she warned.

"I'm not that foolish."

It snowed for two nights and two days without letup, the only change being in intensity. Sometimes Benteen could see across the prairie for a quarter mile, the snow at such times only a powdery sifting, building lazily onto the gradually deepening drifts. The wind had swept clear patches everywhere, and he knew the cattle could still find grass. The south side of the bluffs was better protected than the north, which received the full, direct force of the wind. Then again the wrath of the weather would descend, confining them all indoors.

On the third morning the wind was down, the snow stopped, although now a frost fog hung over the prairie to lend it a silvery frightfulness. Benteen gave day orders to the men at headquarters, then made the slow ride to Sage Creek. He had to pick his way through drifts that covered acres and were belly deep on his horse.

He found things better at the line camp than his lively imagination had pictured them. The wind, Mel Kinder reported, had been fierce but had tended to press the cattle back against the bluffs, keeping them from straying onto enemy range. The line camp was as sturdy a building as the headquarters structures, and the riders hadn't suffered. Benteen had provided them with plenty of extra horses, and so far they were doing fine.

"Kit give us a scare, though," Mel told Benteen on the quiet. "He was gone the night it started, and like to of never got back."

"Gone?" Benteen said, and already knew where.

"You better know it. He does his work fine, gettin' to be a real puncher. But he kites out some nights. Hell of it is, that gal ain't gonna take care of his trouble. I been tellin' Burt we better take the kid to Yellow Bluff and lock Tiger Lily up with him for a week."

"Mel, Scarfield's after the same girl. You've got to keep Kit away from there."

Mel said, "Then we better rope and cut him."

Benteen left orders with Mel to concentrate the outlaw cattle and have them ready to be picked up by the second day thereafter. Riding over he had become convinced that the herd could be driven to Yellow Bluffs and shipped to market. If things got no worse—he kept a wary eye on the dull, vaporous sky.

He swung over to Eph Fadiman's on his way back. He found the nester caught in the same tangle of emotions he himself experienced. Maybe this was a wonderful break—maybe it was a bad one. But Fadiman thought the drive could be made, had to be started at once. They made their plans.

That afternoon the temperature climbed above freezing. That night it fell below zero.

Fadiman was at Bar D an hour after the first murky daylight. The hocks of his horse were bleeding from contact with the broken-glass edges of the ice now sealing the drifts. The snow, melting and then freezing, had been turned deadly overnight.

"This is a fine kettle of fish!" Fadiman exploded. "There ain't a critter on Bitter Creek that could walk five miles in the stuff without gettin' its legs whittled off!"

Benteen nodded somberly. "Looks like we've got to hold up a while."

"I didn't mean that, Nick. I ain't liked the feel of things all fall. Nothin's usual. Too dry last summer. The wild things and Injuns feelin' a hard winter comin'. My old Blackfoot told me he seen a white owl yesterday. The game and the birds is all headin' south. So's he. Mebbe it's now or never."

"I got a feelin' you're right."

"How long would it take?"

Benteen scrubbed a hand over his face, for a moment silent. "There's enough clean grass to keep the critters' strength up, but we'll have to zigzag all the way to get around the drifts. I'd say a week or ten days."

"Out in that stuff," Fadiman said with a groan.

"The alternative is to set tight and see if the weather's bluffing. If we lost we'd have to watch the critters die."

"I'll go on whatever you say."

"Then let's drive as soon as we can get started. I won't be able to take all my boys off the ranch, now. I'd like to have you and Jim, Ad Meadows and Jake Smithwick."

"Glad to do our part," said Fadiman.

They went over the plans they had worked out previously. Benteen wanted to take his horse herd and drive it ahead of the cattle, since horses could handle themselves much better in heavy snow. Also, they could paw down to grass where the steers could not. That would help in the noon and night camps where there was no wind-cleared feed available.

Fadiman had said that Meadows owned a heavy-duty sleigh. This would be substituted for the chuckwagon, and would trail between the horses and the lead cattle. Benteen wanted an extra pair of flankers which, with himself, the cook and wrangler, would make an outfit of eleven men. Fadiman spoke a warning about how the men should dress, of the need for plenty of extra tarpaulins and blankets. Benteen agreed to provision the chuck box out of Bar D's commissary.

They thought they could be ready to trail the following morning.

The day remained clear, with a penetrating cold. As he rode about the range he saw the snow crust was hard, and sometimes the drifts were packed enough to hold up his horse. But where they gave way they were dangerously sharp. And he had a deeper, unabating worry.

There was no doubt that Shannon was keeping a sharp watch on this side of the bluffs. If he saw the outlaws moving out for the railroad, he would know that his death-grip on the nester colony was broken. He would try to break up the drive. Benteen had no doubt of it.

By evening the outlaw beef herd was ready. The crew was picked and prepared to go. The heavy sleigh had been brought up from Ad Meadow's place, the chuck box fitted to it, the vehicle heavily provisioned out of Bar D stores. The horse herd was gathered and being held.

Benteen left Kinder and Friday at the Sage Creek camp but brought Kit in to wrangle on the drive. The kid didn't like the new assignment any better than he had liked being sent over to the north slope, because it kept him away from Cassie. Charlie insisted on cooking for the drive—he had never missed one since he had gone to work for Benteen years before. Benteen meant to leave the new men at Bar D, and Linda would cook for them.

That night the mercury plummeted. Benteen was awakened by the cold and heard the screaming wind, the icy snow grinding the windows with the sound of grain being poured onto paper. He cursed bitterly, silently, and began to feel a sick dread. It did not cause his decision to waver, only strengthened it. The caterpillars, the horses, the Indians, the white owl from the Arctic—they were probably right. The drive had to be made now or Bitter Creek was ruined.

It had been decided that he would ride on to Yellow Bluff the next day to order the stock cars. It would be a tough, all-day trip under present conditions, but he hoped to join and take charge of the drive before it was well away from Bitter Creek. The greasy uneasiness in his stomach grew stronger.

By morning the snow had stopped, and he judged that a couple of inches had fallen. He saddled his blaze horse at once and rode out, with Wad Dennis to take charge of the herd until he had rejoined it. He traveled at fair speed, the wind knifing him in the back as it rushed on.

When he passed the Meadows place at a distance, he regretted that he had asked for Ad in his need for the best men obtainable. Ten days or more would be a long while for Edith to be alone there with her houseful of children, imprisoned, with death roaring across the prairie.

CHAPTER TWELVE

THE BLAZE WAS A TIRED HORSE when it stepped that evening onto the snow-banked streets of Yellow Bluff. Mealy light from the street lamps and the building windows cut into the moody soot of the twilight. Benteen saw only two or three men on the street, hunched and hurrying. He was hungry, so cold his body seemed a dead weight, yet wanted to get his business done before he thought of himself.

He rode at once to the depot and saw with relief that the day's trains had cleared the rails. He stepped into the waiting-room, where hung a guttering light, and for a brief second looked yearningly toward the hot, pot-bellied stove. It smelled of coal, a good smell, at that moment all but intoxicating to him. He stepped to the ticket window, hearing the foreign chatter of the telegraph instrument. A man with an eyeshade and black cuffs was listening, writing on a pad. He kept writing a moment after the instrument stopped its inane talk. Then he looked over and up and saw Benteen.

Having pulled off his stiff gloves, Benteen was working his hands. "Want to order some stock cars," he muttered. "Fifty-sixty. Want 'em here on the sidin' within a week."

The man was staring at him. He said, "You must be Benteen."

His eyes coming up hard against the man's, Benteen said, "That supposed to make a difference?"

"It makes a difference." The telegrapher turned and looked at the instrument on the far desk. It was still quiet. "I just got orders from the division. The road won't carry your cattle, Benteen, till the court's released it from quarantine."

Benteen's stiff hand shot out and clutched the front of the man's shirt. The fellow straightened, worried, then all at once Benteen realized he was only a small cog in a big machine, deciding nothing himself. He released his numbed fingers, drew the arm back.

"How come the company knew I'd be tryin'?" he asked.

The telegrapher looked relieved, almost eager to be as friendly as he dared. "Shannon sent a man in with a telegram to the traffic superintendent. I wired it in this afternoon. Their reply just come in, and my orders, Benteen."

"It's been frozen up four days," Benteen growled. "That quarantine's over."

"No use you tryin' to order cars till you've got a court order that says it's over. They just wouldn't bring 'em in for you."

After a moment Benteen nodded. He turned and walked to the stove, no longer feeling its heat nor smelling the small pleasure of its gaseous coals. The hopelessness of the situation was already apparent. If he tried to get a written release from the court, the thing would be stalled along. Then there would be a threat by the big cattlemen to boycott the railroad if it carried the "outlawed" beef.

That would be effective. A rival line was building through the Black Hills to Belle Fourche, another would soon cross northern Dakota and go up the Missouri to the mountains. They would be competing with the Northern Pacific by another shipping season.

Meanwhile, if the herd came on to Yellow Bluff, it would never be shipped, would die at the river.

Without another look at the company's agent, he walked out of the depot.

What a cinch it had been for Shannon to interpret the activity on Bitter Creek and take his simple step.

But there was a possible way around him, a terrible, crazy gamble.

They had to make the drive to the Dakota badlands after all.

He ate a meal he did not taste, had one drink at the Longhorn against what he had yet to do that night, then stepped back into the saddle. The ferry crossed him back to the river's north bank, the operator muttering, "Much more of this, and I'll have to tie up." Benteen hardly heard him. He put the blaze up the bank and headed north, into the freezing air, and as he rode he felt a bleak, all-consuming urge to kill.

The horse was worn down from the heavy underfooting. Benteen spared it now, knowing the herd was camped somewhere close to Bitter Creek, at the end of its first day's march. He had to reach it before morning, that was all.

The place proved to be the dry wash where he had loitered with Cassie. Benteen reached it before daylight. Charlie had his cooking fire going, the men at the camp were getting dressed, yawning and sluggish with mixed cold and weariness. They stared at Benteen as he rode out of the darkness.

"Man, you got back quick," Fadiman said. "You earned you a night in the hay. How come?"

"We're not shipping cattle at Yellow Bluff," Benteen said bleakly. "Or anywhere else. Shannon beat us to it. He's thrown the weight of the whole stock association against the railroad. They want a court release before they'll even spot cars for the herd. If we went through that rigmarole it would be somethin' else."

"You mean we got to turn around and go home?" Fadiman gasped.

"It's that," said Benteen, "or the drive to Dakota. I told you about Wes Foreman, how he'll take the herd off our hands at a fair price."

"But a hundred miles in this stuff!" Fadiman said with a groan.

"It's that or lose the works. Even if you don't believe

in the signs, this thing just don't feel like a passing storm, boys. At best it means a winter half again as long as usual, mebbe twice as bad."

Ad Meadows said, "Nick's right. We try and keep this herd home all winter we won't only lose it. Everything'll go. Get rid of the herd, and mebbe we could bring through what's left. Benteen, can we drive to Dakota?"

"If we're three times as tough as we figured when we started for Yellow Bluff. It's that much farther."

"I say let's point 'em out. East instead of south."

The other nesters agreed.

Breakfast was eaten quickly, and the men helped Charlie break camp. In the first misty light of dawn the procession moved out, different from any Benteen had ever bossed. Since Fadiman knew the local country and had once been east to Glendive, he broke trail, the hocks of his horse protected against the ice crust by leggings of rawhide. He judged the drifts and shallows, made his best guess as to the way the trail should lie.

Behind followed the horse band, the lead animals likewise legginged, breaking down and packing the snow. Then came the sleigh, and about a hundred yards behind it the first riders and lead steers. Benteen rode point with Wad. They were moving across the wind that morning, a thing a cow horse hated, but the steers had a hard-packed trail to follow. They would have to depend on uncovered grass for feed and quench their thirst with licked snow.

They would have Shannon to fight again. Benteen knew that from the start.

Frost fog lifted to varying heights all across the prairie. In mid-morning it began to clear away, and it seemed to Benteen that the wind had less force. Ahead he could see the snow-trail, the sleigh and horse band, twisting back and forth, sometimes stopping while Fadiman reached a decision about their next tack. A mile ahead and a mile sideways, Benteen thought. But it was the only safe procedure.

The day went better and they covered more ground

than he had dared to hope. They nooned briefly while
Charlie made coffee and passed out chunks of bread, his
fat face apologetic as if the sparse fare was his fault.
He had a fresh beef on the sleigh, frozen solid, for more
nourishing meals at night. He had to melt snow to get
water for the coffee.

All through the afternoon they snailed across the
white, dazzling monotony of prairie. Once Wad called
to Benteen, "Hell, I used to think white was purty. Girls
gettin' married wear it. It's supposed to mean purity,
ain't it? Cold purity. Hell, that's no bargain."

With unerring instinct, Fadiman found a coulee for
the night's camp. There were swept places along its bottom, and a runty growth of cottonwood for Charlie's
fire. The herd was released and all the horses except
those kept up for night work. Benteen helped Charlie
pitch camp. They cut poles and strung a couple of big
tarpaulins out from the sleigh to make a windbreak.

"This is sure refreshin'," Charlie said. "When a man's
spent his life drivin' through blisterin' heat."

"Layered the way you are," Kit said. "All that fat."
He was shivering, blue-faced.

"Well, mebbe for once," Charlie retorted, "you ain't
hot."

The outfit ate supper in the early night. Benteen ordered a double night guard. The immediate danger was
that the cattle and horses might try to hit the back trail
for more familiar surroundings, and the threat of Shannon was always in the back of his mind.

The wind began to mount and grow colder. The canvas on the sleigh and windbreaks began to slap and slat.
The frost fog came in. The fire warmed a space about
itself of some four feet—beyond that there was only the
killing coldness. The men laid out their beds between
the fire and windbreak and began to pull off a few
layers of clothes. These they tried to dry at the fire.

Benteen awakened before it was time to go on guard
with a feeling that he had been frozen solid where he
lay. The fire was still burning, guttering in the wind, a

pot of coffee steaming eternally over it for the men going on and coming off night guard. His blankets, double what he usually used, seemed no protection at all. He could see the other men stirring restlessly, heard somebody curse in a low, bitter voice.

Sounds, he had noticed all that day, were twice as loud as usual. He could hear the movement of horses in the snow, the complaining, restless mutter of the herd. The slapping canvas made a soft but carrying noise.

Cooper and Arno came in presently and called him and Wad. After a cup of coffee that did not warm him, Benteen rode out to the herd. A feeling of hopelessness had begun to work in him, a conviction that long before they reached the Little Missouri men and animals would have been destroyed.

At the end of his trick it began to snow.

He slept no more that night, and he never really warmed up after he got back to bed. They had no thermometer, yet he knew that the temperature was well down past zero. But he wanted it cold now, it had to be the next few days, for the Yellowstone, on its swing to the northeast, would have to be crossed about half way in the drive. Without ice able to hold up the herd, he didn't know how they could do it.

Out on the prairie he could hear horses hammering the ground, pawing down to grass. The snow kept falling so that, looking out from under the blankets that protected his head, he could see its fat, settling flakes between him and the fire. A man started coughing, maybe from the frosted air slicing into his lungs. Benteen worried about that. When it got cold enough, air could be like fire in the lungs of men and horses breathing from heavy exertion.

The drive pushed out in the snow and all through that morning moved in a little private world that knew only snow and wind and the aching cold. Benteen's feet felt like blocks of ice in the stirrups. In mid-afternoon the wind shifted slightly, or else Fadiman lost his sense of direction. It came head-on, the stinging particles of snow grinding into the faces of the men and animals.

Benteen was on the point of riding ahead to check with Fadiman—he had hardly seen the forward sleigh and cavvy all day—when the lead steers balked. Just stopped in their tracks and refused to go on in the face of the fearful wind. The cursing of punchers—loud in the cold—informed him of the file's complete stopping, steer by steer.

"Hell—if they bull back on us!" Wad shouted. "If they've decided home couldn't be worse than this!"

"Get 'em movin'!" Benteen roared.

The leaders stood still and stolid on the hard-packed trail. They wouldn't budge, Benteen and Wad drove their horses at them, cursed them blue, finally began shooting their guns. The steers started to turn in their tracks, all along the line to where it vanished in the grim curtain of snow. In a moment they would start to move that way, which would mean that the drag—suddenly in the lead—had bolted. He could hear men shouting back there but dared not ride off to see what was happening.

Once again he and Wad plunged their horses into the lead cattle. That time an old steer moved forward a little. Benteen whacked it across the rump and it sprang ahead. He yelled and kept crowding it. It kept going, almost trotting suddenly. The steers behind closed up. In a moment the point was again in motion. The file began to come on out of the snow behind.

Benteen's heart was thundering. As soon as he was sure the line would keep moving, he spoke to Wad, then rode ahead to find Fadiman.

He passed the sleigh, Charlie staring at him numbly from its seat, then Kit and the horse band. Fadiman was just ahead, riding uneasily. He gave a start when Benteen came up to him.

"Glad you showed!" he called through the wind. "I've zigged and zagged so damned much I've lost my bearin's."

"You're headin' into the wind."

"Know it, but I figuré we got to. There was a deep drift back there where I turned. Mebbe a coulee. My horse sunk to its belly."

"They tried to bull on us. They won't face the wind much longer."

"If this is a coulee and we can get down into it to camp, we better do it."

"You stay with the cavvy," Benteen decided. "I'll see what I can find out."

He sent his horse forward into the unbroken snow, and without anybody ahead of him now felt alone in a lost and eerie world. All the working horses wore rawhide to protect their legs, but the new snow now overlying the crust held the blaze up. He crowded the horse to the right, and all at once it was dropping down a decline.

The wind was soon less strong in its rush against him. Fadiman had judged correctly; he had dropped down into some kind of sheltered bottomland. He kept riding, and a little later came to a stand of trees. He felt some relief, although it meant a shortened day of trailing. In that blinding snow the herd could run into sudden death any minute.

He retraced his horse's tracks until he came to Fadiman. "Your hunch was right. Wood down there, and it's warmer. You can follow my tracks. I better get back and help Wad. Havin' bulled back once, the critters are apt to get the habit."

An hour later the herd was turned loose in the storm to rustle for grass. The camp was set up again by the trees. Charlie thawed out the mulligan he had made the night before, thawed and fried meat. With the tarpaulins reducing the already lessened wind, the camp was almost cheerful in comparison to the one the night before.

It stopped snowing in the night and, on his night guard, Benteen watched the black overhead split raggedly to let a little moonlight show. At daylight he saw that they were in a pothole. The steers did not want to leave its relative comfort, and Kit was bringing the horse herd in.

Fadiman estimated that morning that the Yellowstone was still ten day's drive from them.

Benteen was worried about the country that lay beyond the river; when approached from this direction it was strange to them all. If the weather remained clear enough, he could scout it out, but the question of available grass troubled him. He knew there were many hay ranches all through the valley bottom, and decided to ride ahead before they reached it and see if he could buy a stack or two. They could break ice from the river to get water which cattle have to have when they eat hay. It would probably pay them to lie up two or three days to recruit the animals.

They trailed on, always east and a little south, always at a slow, wearing pace through a killing monotony of cold and whiteness.

CHAPTER THIRTEEN

BENTEEN LOOKED DOWN AT LAST upon the Yellowstone from a cold, windy knob. The valley was broad here, as was the water. Immediately below him the land fell away, piled and blown and rounded by the eternal snow. Frost fog hung over the lowland, heavier above the water but here and there torn so that he could make out two things that interested him. First were what he was sure were the structures of some ranch, probably one of the hay outfits Fadiman had mentioned. And from this distance, at a place where the fog curtain had lifted a little, was what he thought to be the glint of river ice.

The wind knifed him through the sheepskin, his two shirts and two suits of underwear. He had his hat brim tied down about his ears by a piece of cloth, yet the flesh of the ears was beyond feeling. He could not remember how long it had been that his feet were numbed lumps of cold.

He scanned the immediate foreground, looking for a place to descend. It seemed possible anywhere, an aspect he did not trust, for the softness and gentle rolling of the snow was insidiously deceptive. He rode a short way to the south and around a rocky point saw swept ground that looked safe. He put the horse down the decline to the bottom, paused again to get his bearings in the fog suddenly surrounding him, then rode out toward the river.

He reached the water and, as nearly as he could determine, the heavy, frozen sheet of ice at the bank ran clear across. It had to be that way. Otherwise the cattle were trapped on this side. He rode on, coming to a fence and following it until he made out a barn. A moment afterward he was in the yard of a place that could have been one of the nester setups on Bitter Creek.

He halloed the house as he rode in. When he reached the porch he saw a man standing there, staring out into the vapory atmosphere in curiosity. The fellow wore an old buffalo coat, a fur cap, and behind the immediate interest in his face was uneasiness.

"Howdy," Benteen said. "It's a cold day."

"A cold week or so, stranger." He was wary all right, watching Benteen intently. He made no invitation to light down and come in. As Benteen swung out of leather anyhow, the man stiffened his body under the big coat. He seemed about to speak a warning.

Benteen only wanted to warm himself. Trailing the reins of his horse, he slapped his arms across his body, stomped his feet without feeling a thing.

"I got a herd comin' on," said Benteen. "I'm wonderin' if I could buy hay around here."

"Hay?" the man said sharply. His face was angry suddenly. "What the hell you doin' with a herd out here right now?"

"Trailin' east. You got hay?"

"I had hay," the man said bitterly. "Up to yesterday. Three stacks that some sons of bitches set fire to the night before."

Benteen quit rubbing his arms, his eyes slapping the man in the shock of that disclosure. The fellow meant it; temper was up full in him, with a continuing uneasiness about this visitor.

"I'll be damned," Benteen breathed. "And mebbe I'm responsible, friend, though not the way you think. My herd isn't rustled, if that's what you're wondering. And I sure as hell wouldn't burn up hay I need bad. Somebody's tryin' to stop me, that's all. Tryin' hard."

The man's face changed a little. He jerked his head and said, "Come on in and get warm."

The place was a plain, one-room shanty, and the fellow seemed to live there alone. He gave the name of Murdy when Benteen volunteered his own. They got out of their coats, and Murdy poked up the fire in the room's one stove. He took the black, battered coffee pot off the stove and filled two tin cups. Benteen tried to roll a cigarette but his fingers were too stiff to work.

"Let me do that for you," Murdy said. He sounded friendlier but said no more until he had rolled a cigarette and handed it to Benteen. "So that's it, and it's the first time there's been any sense to the damned thing. My hay ain't all that went up in smoke. My neighbor up the river lost two stacks. The one down lost four. And that's all the hay there is in this stretch of the valley, Benteen. It sure leaves us in a tight fix."

Benteen took a sip of the hot coffee; its feeling and taste were a wild delight. "Then mebbe you'll help me deal with the men responsible."

"Hell, they must have dragged their freight. I would of if I'd burned some poor man's hay."

Benteen shook his head. "They're still around. They don't mean to let me get the herd over the river till it's thawed and the ice rotted. Then I'll be pinned down here till the next freeze. By that time the critters might be too weak to make it where we're goin'. Is there any place around here men could hole up without being found very easy?"

Murdy scratched his bushy head for a moment. "Why, there's an old trapper's shack t'other side of the river."

"Then they're over there. Probably patroling the river on that side to spot me when I show here with the cattle. Ticklish job gettin' steers to cross ice. They figure they can bust it up and keep it busted up, dead easy."

Murdy's worry returned, heavier, more crowding than before. "There'll sure be a mess if you do get trapped here. Us settlers'll have all we can do to winter our livestock the way it is."

"I don't figure to get trapped, Murdy. I'm sure sorry about your hay, but mebbe I can at least help square it for you. Thanks for the coffee and the tip about their hangout."

"You goin' over there?" the man asked incredulously.

Benteen shook his head. "I'd rather catch 'em all together, and right now they're probably ridin' the river over there, waiting for us to hit this side somewhere."

The hot coffee felt good in his belly when presently he swung back into the saddle. The old fury seemed to add to his body heat. Shannon's spy system had kept working. He must have got men here by way of the railroad for them to have burned those haystacks two nights ago.

There was no doubt that a determined effort would be made to trap the cattle here at the valley or else force their return to Bitter Creek. Once the ice had started to rot, a man would be foolish to venture onto it even on a horse. A real chinook and thaw could not melt the ice sufficiently, at that stage, to permit swimming.

This unseasonable cold seemed more apt to break up than to continue without letup so that it might be a month or six weeks before a freeze came of sufficient intensity to permit escape.

As he climbed back out of the valley, Benteen's mind was heavy with the problem of meeting the situation. Crossing would be slow at best, and there was little chance that he could move up or down the river without being detected. He didn't want it that way, really. He wanted to know who Shannon had sent on this mission, to have it out with them.

He found the herd five miles out on his back trail, coming on doggedly through the gray forenoon. He told Fadiman grimly of what he had learned and, as he talked, watched the nester's face change to a bitter defiance.

"That lousy son of a buck has got all the advantages!" Fadiman burst out.

"We've got one," Benteen answered. "We have a fair idea of what they'll try to do."

"And what's to stop 'em from doin' it? That bull back we had the other day is nothin' to what it'll be like trying to get steers out onto ice with bullets whangin' at 'em from across."

"We've got to stop the bullets, Eph."

"Can we?"

"I dunno. We'll try."

The herd kept on. Benteen's path that morning had laid out the easiest route for it; now there was need only to follow the tracks of his horse. They were still short of the river by two or three miles when they halted briefly to noon. Then they went on.

When again he was on the point above the river, Benteen saw that the fog had lifted. Now the Yellowstone lay below him as one broad ribbon of glinting ice. He could see no one on the far shore, but anybody spying would take pains to keep concealed with the visibility now good. That didn't matter; he wanted Shannon's men to know that the herd had arrived.

They dropped into the valley, then moved upriver for some three miles so as not to hold the cattle on Murdy's private domain. Charlie pitched camp, while the steers were allowed to drift upstream in their eternal search for grass while being held back on the lower side. They had to be watched on the river side, too, since they might wander to some air pocket for water and slide in. There was an hour or two of daylight left. Benteen used them in riding along the bank, picking the place for the crossing.

He chose a point where a sand bar ran out into the water, and his interest was as much in the sand as in the narrowed sheet of ice the bar created between itself and the opposite bank. There was an undercut place in the bank where sand could be dug out. It had been sufficiently dry at the start of the freeze so that it had not hardened in a surface crust. He kicked a little of it with his foot to make sure.

He got back to the camp in time for supper. The men sat about in their hunched, unending coldness, plates of steaming food on their laps which they tried to fork up with numbed hands. They were a wild looking lot, he thought, their cheekbones blackened with soot against snow blindness, beards below that, and the rest of their heads and bodies bundled into a grotesque fatness.

He explained the situation briefly, concluding, "In the morning we'll lift the chuck box off the sleigh and unload the other stuff. We've got to sand us a path clear across for the critters to walk on. I don't think Shannon's hyenas'll interfere with that. Better to try and surprise us when we get the herd out a ways onto the ice. But they'll be there on the other side, watchin' everything. Shannon would send a pretty strong force. I'd like to have a volunteer to help me hand 'em a little surprise."

He had his pick of every man there.

Benteen chose Wad Dennis. The plan made, the decision reached, his mind stopped its churning. The men hugged the fire and tried to get warm, an impossibility in the perpetual wind. They dreamed their secret dreams, and Benteen supposed that these might be of the sun-drenched plains of Texas, when it came to his own men, and the hearths of home for the nesters. They were good men, fighting men, little men of big stature.

They spent the next day sanding a forty-foot path across the river. At first the sleigh was backed out from the shore, men scattering the sand from the rear to provide footing for the horses. Afterward, as they widened and built this up, the work went more swiftly. Benteen passed back and forth, never openly studying the eastern shore but watching it always. He saw nothing to suggest the men somewhere close who were bent on breaking up the crossing.

In mid-afternoon the temperature began to rise. Benteen noticed it when he grew aware that for the first time since leaving Bar D he was actually warm all over. The realization tightened his nerves another notch. They had no time to delay. He had planned on waiting until the next day to attempt the crossing. By then it might be too late.

Returned to the west bank, he issued brief orders. The herd was to be rounded in and pointed at the sand trail, signaling that the big effort was about to start. But the cattle would not be started for one hour. This delay would be made to seem natural by the men's helping to break camp and load up the sleigh.

He and Wad each took two extra blankets, then rode out of the valley along the broad path packed by the cavvy and herd coming in. Out of sight of the river, they turned south immediately, moving upstream. They went on, silent, for nearly a mile. Then they let themselves down to the river edge again.

It was a slow job crossing the horses, but Benteen wanted them. He and Wad moved onto the ice first, laying the blankets end to end, then leading the horses out to the edge of the farthermost. Then the process would be repeated, the horses given a secure underfooting and coming willingly. There was still a strong light left when they reached the other shore.

Wad said, "Now to get in behind the devils and heat their rumps with some hot lead."

"This time we shoot to kill."

They rode straight away from the river and, as Benteen had expected, were not long in cutting the sign of a large party of riders, moving downstream. Benteen judged that there were half a dozen men, moving slowly. He and Wad exchanged bleak looks of satisfaction. They rode on until just short of the place where Benteen judged the sand track touched this bank. Then, dismounting, they left the horses and continued, tramping through the snow.

They came at once upon the other horses, and there were the six Benteen had guessed. Their brands were strange to him, but he had already guessed that Shannon must have sent this force by train, and the mounts would have been secured at some railroad town near this point.

The men had moved away from their horses by crawling through the snow. Benteen judged that he and Wad had spent most of their hour in getting here. In a whisper, he said, "We'll each get on a quarter to 'em to keep 'em pinned down. Not too close. Let me open it, and after I do it's got to be fast and furious."

"If you can deliver the speed, I've got the fury."

Benteen smiled. He and Wad might both be dead in another ten minutes, but the man was ready to laugh. He went on, and a moment later they were both crawling through the snow.

Benteen feared the sound of his dragging hands and knees would carry to the edge of the river in the magnified loudness of the cold. There was open land on both sides of the river, and there would be nothing but snow for protection once the fight was on. He soon topped over the slight rise in the ground, could see below. He halted, pressed flat, watching downward with steady care. From this point there seemed to be only an unbroken whiteness, clear down to the water, but he knew that his foes were there.

He waited in shallow breathing for what seemed an interminable time. Then he could tell from the activity across the river that the crew was getting ready to start. A little point of lead steers stretched from the main herd to the start of the sand path. A couple of riders moved their horses down closer to it. They seemed to call something back and forth, then moved in upon the pointers.

The puzzled animals milled a little and tossed their heads. Somebody's rope end went to work, then a steer let itself be forced out onto the sand. In a moment two others followed it, sniffing the sand, stepping carefully. All at once the herd was moving out onto the ice.

Benteen's ears registered the shallow but crashing run of his heart as he waited in an agony of tension. The herd was not as yet in bullet range. But those leaders were a trigger, connected mentally to the tight nervous systems of the men intending to throw them back. Benteen waited for it to work, then it did.

The sharp, punching crack of a pistol shot rang out. Benteen instantly threw a bullet into the place where he had seen the puff of smoke. A man let out a scream.

They came up together, staggered men suddenly in panic. Benteen stayed flat, as did Wad. But their guns kicked their palms as thunder cut the chilled atmosphere. A man toppled over, another. Benteen had by then recognized Buck Potter, Frisbee and Cornell—men who had once before felt his anger but who had had plenty of time to recover.

Scarfield, still Shannon's big gun, was not along.

But Potter seemed bent on redeeming himself for his former failure. He had dropped flat already, as had Cornell and Frisbee. They had been forced to turn their backs on the river, but they began to shoot furiously. Then, across the river, the two point riders moved out farther onto the sand trail. They got in close enough to begin to put shots behind the Shannon trio. At that range they had only a worrying effect.

"You ready to quit?" Benteen shouted.

They could not again, after their previous humiliation. They came up fighting, knowing that only through a rush could they hope to break out. That gave them elevation to see Benteen and Wad. Bullets threw snow into Benteen's face. He got up on one knee. He could feel a slug tear close to his battened hat as he shot. Forward a man went down. The others flattened, and a close-whining bullet drove Benteen down likewise.

A sense of futility washed through him as he remembered the rising temperature. If these men managed to hold out, simply keeping the herd from crossing long enough, this higher temperature would do the rest of their work for them, indefinitely pinning the cattle on the other side without feed. That was still their hope, and the reason why they had forted up again after that first surprised outbreak of panic.

He risked a look to see that the herd was still halted,

the punchers with it not daring to risk it on the soften-
ing ice until the dispute on the other shore was settled.
The riders who had come part way over were still throwing shots into the snow but doing little good. They
kept him and Wad from crawling in closer.

"Potter!" he yelled. "You better give up! Longer you
wait, the harder we'll make it on you!"

"The hell with you, Benteen!"

He lifted himself slightly, hoping he had placed Potter's voice close enough to lay in a good shot. Someone
else had the same idea because, even as he exerted himself, something slammed his head so hard his vision
streaked with fire. He let out a groan and sagged limp,
his strength completely gone from him. If the man who
had creased him knew it, he realized vaguely, he would
move in for the kill, and Wad was done for too. He
fought desperately to hold onto himself.

He was still dazed when he forced himself up, heedless of everything except the fact that without his help
Wad couldn't hold them off. And then he saw the man
slithering toward him through the snow. Benteen shot,
drawing on all the training of the years to do it for
him mechanically. The man pulled into a hunch and
rolled over. Benteen forced himself to stand.

His chattering gun forced them to roll and twist and
over on his right Dennis shoved up. Benteen kept the
Shannon men stirring while Wad laid in more clear-
headed shots. A man threw up his arms and fell side-
wise, another let out a yell of surrender and shoved
up his hands.

Dennis went slogging in and took their guns. Benteen
sagged in the snow, waiting for his brain to stop reeling.
He didn't know how long it was afterward when he
opened his eyes and could see. Wad was standing with
his sixgun covering two prisoners. They were Con Shannon's cheapest gunhands, Cornell and Frisbee.

"Rest are done for," Wad called, "including Potter."

Leaving the prisoners with Wad, Benteen stumbled
down to the river and motioned for the herd to come

on, the thought burning in his aching head that there still was no time to waste.

Afterward, his scalp wound dressed, Benteen took the prisoners to Murdy's place and left them to be turned over to the sheriff.

They camped that night on the east bank of the river, where they had their first warm sleep since leaving Bitter Creek. The next day was clear, the sun came out, the temperature stayed above freezing. Yet it did not thaw sufficiently to slow their progress.

Two weeks later they delivered the herd on the Little Missouri and accepted Wes Foreman's checks. Then riders and horse band started home, able to travel much faster.

They were men of mixed moods. Ad Meadows expressed one sentiment: "Beef checks, by God! And just before Christmas! When me and the missus was worried sick about what we could do for the kids! Boys, I'm goin' to Yellow Bluff when we get home and blow a little piece of my new dinero."

Eph Fadiman, failing to share that elation, shook his head. "If it wasn't for my family there, mebbe I wouldn't even want to go home. We ain't licked Shannon, boys, and don't get that notion. A setback only makes him worse, as we've found out. We've got plenty of steers yet to get through what sure looks like a mean winter so far. I sure don't feel easy in my mind."

And Benteen knew Eph was right.

CHAPTER FOURTEEN

On the December day when the trail outfit reached Bitter Creek the temperature stood at freezing. There had been several snows since the first one nearly a month before; snow lay on the range at an average depth of one foot but was alternately scoured and drifted until the prairie was a mixture of life-giving grass and death traps.

But Fadiman's Blackfoot had fled south with many another of his race, much of the game was gone, and every now and then somebody saw one of the rare white owls from the Arctic. The decampers had seen them previously and had taken them as an omen to vanish.

Benteen, as he settled back into ranch work, was host to a twin feeling: bitterness and satisfaction. In his relentless drive against Bitter Creek, Shannon had forced it into a position of strength greater than before. The salting and judicious use of grass, before the onslaught of winter, had conserved the supply as never before. The sale of cattle to Foreman had reduced the nester herds until now there was a good chance to bring them through even a severe winter.

Moreover, the range south of Buffalo Bluffs was more protected from the killing north wind than was the Sage Creek side. Shannon himself had fenced the gaps, save for the one at Bar D, so that his cattle were inclined to stray into them and there halt miserably, without water or grass.

One night while he sat with Linda in the ranch house living-room, Benteen said, "All Shannon needs to do now is force us to drive wells to insure plenty of water and we'll have the choice part of the whole country."

"Wells?" she asked.

"I've thought a lot about that," he told her. "Down on the Pecos plain they're discoverin' that dry country can have all kinds of water under the surface. Depends on the formation. It makes sense. If water don't run off on top, then it must have to run off underneath."

"Wells are hard work."

Benteen shook his head. "Just expensive. They're diggin' 'em with churn drills, goin' down a long ways. But when they hit water at all, they usually get plenty. Wind pumps and tanks do the rest."

"You've proved we have plenty of grass," Linda mused. "And you could make wells do what the salt did, couldn't you? Spot them in places where the cattle wouldn't range otherwise. Nick, you kind of amaze me."

"Is that all?"

Her cheeks colored and she looked away. Her excitement when he reappeared from the drive had been too great to hide. He had hoped it was something more than just the general elation and relief they all had felt. Otherwise she had remained as before, a woman of subtle provocation with a rock wall she could raise up between them in jig time.

As he went to the bunkhouse to turn in, Benteen was thinking of Christmas, now only two days away. In Fallon on the way home he had bought a present for her, a gold watch to be pinned on her blouse. Maybe it was extravagant, in bad taste, but that was the way he felt about her. And at times he had caught her working with knitting needles on something she always hid quickly when he came to the house.

It was a good time of year. He didn't want to hate anybody just then, and he wondered if the weather would permit some kind of a whooperoo at Bar D for the settlement. He mentioned it to Fadiman, who mentioned it to others, and the thing was decided spontaneously. The Bar D outfit went to work with a will, fixing up the ranch dining-room. Charlie, waddling and enormously beatific, worked long and temperamentally in his kitchen.

Kit and Wad rode off some place and were gone all day. Since Wad was along, Benteen didn't worry, but he kept thinking of Cassie and the month Kit had been away. The two punchers were back in late afternoon dragging great bundles of pine boughs found up where the wood had been cut. When his establishment was thus decorated, pungent and pleasant, Charlie was so moved he served some of the doughnuts he had made for the party.

Benteen wondered if word of the Christmas party had reached Cassie. He didn't want to see her, to dodge her all evening, but knew it would be unkind and unfair to leave her out. He decided to leave that up to Fadiman, who had spread the word and who would feel the same way about her.

Jim Damon came by in mid-afternoon. He was heading for Yellow Bluff to spend the holiday with Helen and her mother. He was an excited, happy looking man as, after doughnuts and coffee, he rode on. He had got a little beef money, after all. Benteen suspected that wedding plans would be made before Jim rode back to Bitter Creek.

The nester families began to come in shortly after dark, some on horseback, some in jumper sleighs. Simultaneously it began to snow again.

"The hell with it!" Jake Smithwick shouted. "Let's eat Charlie's oyster supper!"

The snow didn't look threatening, was only a fine sifting gently stirred by the wind. The noise of the children and grown-up talk filled the whole mess-house, women marveled at Charlie's fixings—then Cassie arrived with Bullnose Wells and his wife. Bullnose looked unhappy about it, but the women probably had made him come.

"That's everybody except Ad and Edith," Fadiman said happily to Benteen. "Ad went to town with the sleigh yesterday, but they'll be here. Edith was some excited. She loves a party. Did you know she can do a square dance on that crutch?"

"In my book," said Benteen, "she'll do at anything you care to mention, Eph."

"You're right there."

The large Meadows family still had not arrived when supper had been eaten. Then, an hour afterward, Ad's oldest girl showed up alone. She looked frightened.

"Ma's worried about Pa," she said. "He ain't got home yet."

Benteen's straying eyes found Fadiman's.

"I don't reckon there's a thing to worry about, Cathy," Fadiman said gently.

Cathy began to cry.

Benteen stood at the door looking out. The snow didn't seem much heavier, certainly not of sufficient force to hold Ad up on the road. Thirty miles on a primitive, snow-choked road made slow going, that was all. Yet he was uneasy, maybe because Cathy had not been able to keep back her tears. He moved on outside, pulling the door shut behind him.

He was in the bunkhouse getting into his sheepskin when Fadiman stepped in.

"You remembered what I did," Fadiman said. "Shannon."

Benteen nodded.

"I'm goin' with you."

"If you want," Benteen agreed.

They were soon riding south along the Yellow Bluff road, the snowfall not enough to slow them down. They went silently, neither man caring to voice the sudden sick color of his thinking. Shannon had been set back on his heels every time he braced Bitter Creek. It was time he acted again.

Then this all seemed foolish when they came to the Meadows turn-off.

"There's his tracks!" Fadiman shouted, pointing down at the road ahead. "He's home!"

Benteen could make out the newly cut grooves of
the sleigh runners where they turned in toward the distant ranch house. Grinning, he said, "Mebbe we better
not make fools of ourselves by goin' on in. They'll be
at the party pretty soon."

"We better tell Edith Cathy made it to your place
all right."

They rode on in, out of custom shouting toward the
house as they approached. Benteen saw the light where
a door opened immediately. The sleigh had pulled on
past the house toward the barn door and was still
hitched to the team. They planned on leaving for Bar
D, Benteen reflected.

It was Edith who hobbled to the edge of the porch.
She was screaming.

Benteen dug spurs and sent his horse floundering
forward. Fadiman surged behind him.

"Thank God you got here!" Edith said. "The sleigh
come home—Ad—he wasn't in it—"

Benteen had a sense of the whole scene being swept
away by a smashing fist. Something deep in his spine
hurt acutely. Flinging out of the saddle, he ran to her.
She collapsed against him and made a dry sob. Frightened children stared out through the open door.

"Stay here with her, Nick," Fadiman shouted. "I'm
goin' on!"

"I'm all right," Edith muttered. "Both of you go—
find him—"

"How long have the horses been here?" Benteen asked
quietly.

"Just a few minutes. I was going to ride to Bar D but
I couldn't leave the children alone. I hoped somebody
would come. Go now. Please." Edith Meadows turned,
in control of herself again, and swung herself back
indoors.

"It's happened," Fadiman said in a low, torn voice.
"Another murder. Sure as God made little green ap-
ples."

"We won't know till we see."

They went on, rushing their horses now, forcing them recklessly across the snow. The prairie was open for a long ways, and they saw nothing lying in the snow beside the road. But Benteen's fear was growing: Damon had passed along this road recently, too—alone.

They had nearly passed the lone cottonwood standing at a distance beside the trail when Fadiman pointed suddenly.

"My God, Nick— Look!"

Benteen had already seen it, now that they were abreast of the tree, the dangling body of a man who stared upward through the leafless limbs of the old tree.

They rode over slowly. Then Fadiman turned his head and vomited.

They cut Ad Meadows down and straightened him out on the snow, neither saying anything, neither really living themselves. A sleighload of Christmas things for his family . . . The red yeast of rage mounted in Benteen. They put Meadows across Fadiman's saddle, and the nester swung up behind Benteen.

"Your place, Nick," Fadiman said. "I better send Bessie to Edith."

At last Benteen voiced his other fear. "I wonder about Jim."

"No tellin'. Ad must of been pretty late if the horses just got home. Jim was a long ways past here by then. Him and Ad must of met somewheres on the road."

"No use ridin' all the way to Yellow Bluff to find out, I guess," Benteen reflected.

"My God, Nick—what does it mean?"

Benteen didn't answer, but he knew. Shannon realized that Bitter Creek had managed itself so as to stand a good chance of surviving the winter. Now Scarfield had stepped back into the picture. This was the kind of thing he would do—for pay.

There had been that talk about rustling at the stock association meeting where the nesters had been outlawed. Shannon had started it, preparing himself. Once, way back there, he had said something about the next time they'd use rope—that day when he had tried to keep the throughs from coming into the county. Suddenly it was a clear and ugly picture in Benteen's mind.

The Christmas party at Bar D had already lost its gaiety. When Benteen stepped in, black-featured, snow-dusted, he knew there was no use hiding a thing. He spoke in a clipped, flat voice.

"Ad's dead. Murdered. Hung."

There was only Cathy Meadows's sudden wail.

Several of the women left in Fadiman's jumper sleigh, Linda with them, heading for the Meadows place. They took the stricken Cathy. Afterward hard-eyed men stared at Benteen.

Finally Jake Smithwick said, "Shannon. No doubt of it. Same as there was no doubt he had Einer killed. Boys, it's time we hung Con Shannon."

Benteen had expected that; he could feel it pushing at him from everywhere in the room.

"I'm going over to Slash S in the morning," he said. "Leave it to me. You've got to." His eyes raked to Bull-nose Wells, to Cassie. "Your friend Scarfield did the job."

"He's not my friend!"

"Then tell Ira about this. He's makin' sell-out talk, and this hangin' is supposed to spread that spirit. Tell him if he sells to Shannon instead of me, I'll kill him on sight. You, too, Bullnose. Now, I reckon we can spare your company."

But they all left, then. There was nothing else to do.

Benteen sent Wad to Yellow Bluff, not only to check on Damon but to wire the sheriff. Afterward, alone with his own men, he paced the floor. The storm began to pinch up in intensity, the wind was howling now. Ad's body was over in the ranch house, in what had once been Einer's bed. Charlie had gone over there quietly to sit with the dead man.

Daylight came. The storm was down a little, and Benteen saddled a horse and rode out.

Cooper and Friday were at the Sage Creek camp now. Benteen stopped there for coffee and a bite of breakfast. Then he rode on down the creek. He had never before been at Slash S headquarters. But he came upon the place easily three hours later. It was a big establishment, he saw at once, using both sides of the creek. He rode into the ranch compound unhurriedly.

The place looked deserted, but it was the mounting cold that kept everyone indoors. Benteen rode to the big house steps, swung down and dropped the reins to the snow. He climbed the steps, reached the door and rapped hard. It opened a moment later, and Con Shannon stood there.

He was dressed but his hair was still tousled, as if he had just got out of bed. He must have expected one of his men for the slackness of his face vanished as muscles jerked.

"You!"

"Me. And I don't figure to stay long, Shannon. Just long enough to tell you we found Ad Meadows. And mebbe to put a slug in your guts."

The muscles kept jerking. "What about Meadows?"

"Naturally you don't know he was hung last night by Scarfield and probably a few of your men. There were plenty of horse tracks around there, even if they are snowed under by now."

"How do you know it was Scarfield?" Shannon demanded. "And if it was him, why tie him to me?"

Benteen laughed. "The nesters wanted to organize a hangin' bee for you, Shannon. I talked 'em out of it. I aim to settle for Ad and Einer myself."

In sudden bitterness, Shannon said, "I don't know any more than you do about either man. But there's one thing I'm sure of. If Meadows was strung up, he had it comin'. After you pulled your outlaw roundup, we found plenty of Sage Creek cows still bein' followed by calves wearin' Bitter Creek brands. Your nesters sure kept their runnin' irons busy while they was over here on our range. We can prove it. Meadow's brand

was one we found, Jim Damon's another. So don't try
nothin', Benteen. This country won't heat up much
over what happened to Meadows."

Benteen had the feeling of hot metal in his belly.
They had already arranged their phony rustling evidence. It would be exactly as Shannon claimed. Nobody
except friends and relatives got excited over the hanging of a rustler.

Savagely he said, "I'm gonna get you, Shannon, and
I'm gonna get Scarfield. Tell him that. Tell him I want
to know if he's got the courage to let me come up to
him."

"Your threats'll only count against you."

Benteen turned his back and walked down to his
waiting horse.

CHAPTER FIFTEEN

THE NEW STORM was unrelenting except for a few hours, when Ad Meadows was buried. By the time Jess Wilson reached Bitter Creek there wasn't a trace of physical evidence on the blown prairie. He got nowhere. Nobody had expected him to, and the sheriff turned with more interest to the matter of the gunfight on the Yellowstone. Murdy and his settler neighbors had been insistent and vehement in their claim that Shannon's men had burned the haystacks and contested the river crossing and started the shooting. When he had heard Benteen's account of it, Wilson shrugged, forced to drop the matter.

Benteen sent Wad Dennis down to Meadows's place to take over Ad's work, and Wad went willingly. Jim Damon returned from Yellow Bluff. The death of Meadows had been a shock to him—he had met Ad on the town trail probably not over two hours before it happened. Ad had been a happy man at that point, with toys and Christmas fixings for his family.

"I got to tell you something, Jim," Benteen said. "Watch yourself. Shannon mentioned your name along with Ad's. I know why he picked you two. You tended camp and watched the cavvy and beef cut during the roundup. You had time to brand a few of their calves. None of the rest of us could swear you didn't. I'm afraid you're next on the list."

"Let 'em try," Damon growled.

"Don't take that attitude," Benteen warned. "They wouldn't give you an even chance. And I figured you and Helen might tie up pretty soon since you sold some beef."

"That's right. But it ain't goin' to make me tuck my tail between my legs."

"Of course not. Just don't take any chances you don't have to."

Damon's face darkened. "We got to smoke out that Scarfield and fix him, even if Shannon himself is too dangerous to touch right now. Because I won't be the only one. Shannon must hope to scare most of us into sellin'. Otherwise he wouldn't have picked a thing like hangin' for Ad. When he finds it won't work, it won't only be me. He can manufacture rustlin' evidence against anybody he chooses, and the whole damned county would back him."

"That's how it stacks up," Benteen agreed.

Scarfield was his own problem, yet he could think of no way to force the man to face a showdown. Killing was his business, and even if Shannon passed on the taunt Benteen had made at Slash S, Scarfield would not let his vanity interfere with his profits.

There was a chance of trapping the man at Glade's. The bait of Cassie must still be strong whether or not she was accommodating the man. Yet Benteen could arrive at no method of timing it so the killer would not be warned. Meanwhile, until he could bring that about or find a sane way to go after Shannon, Bitter Creek had to rely on vigilance.

The storm promised to help. It snowed intermittently through the first week of January. On the ninth day it fell in earnest for sixteen continuous hours, each hour laying an inch of new snow on the prairie pack. The temperature dropped until the ranch thermometer stood at thirty below zero. It stayed at that mark or lower when the storm abated, although it continued to snow off and on.

During one bitter, stormbound day Benteen went over to the ranch house to see how Linda was managing. The events alone or the storm alone would be punishing enough to human nerves. As he came into the warm room he sensed at once her high emotional tension. He hadn't meant to stay but now he pulled off his coat and hung it up with his hat. She needed company, needed it badly.

"Got a checker board?" he said, grinning at her.

"I don't want to play checkers."

"Poker?"

She frowned in distaste.

He moved across to where she sat by the fire, put a finger under her chin and made her look up at him. "You're brooding, and that never does any good."

"Who wouldn't brood?" she said sharply. "For that matter, what's any good?"

Her vehemence sobered him. He had to get her mind off Ad and Edith, off Shannon—maybe off Cassie. "Lots of things," he said mildly, "when a girl's as young, as pretty and as wonderful as you are."

In a sudden fury, she said, "Don't say things like that to me!"

"Ah," he said. "Do you think I asked Cassie to the party?"

"Why should I wonder? Why should I care?"

"Because," said Benteen, "you could love me as I love you if you'd let yourself."

She turned her face away from him.

"You think I went overboard with Cassie," he continued. "And you're dead right. I did. Now you can quit tearing the question to pieces in your mind."

She swung back toward him. "I never doubted it. There's no doubt that she'd be willing. Come to think of it, no real reason to suppose that you wouldn't be, too."

He saw how deeply the thing had eaten into her, remembered her reverence for the love that had been between Ad and Edith. She had wanted that, had supposed that it was possible for herself. Now it seemed to her that he had not felt the decent things between them that she must have felt. He had slapped her, all right, smack in the face with Cassie.

"There've been other women, too," he said. "A man gets hungry, Linda. You probably know that but don't really understand it yet. And there can come a moment when things take over, that's all."

"I can't imagine them taking me over."

"You can't imagine it, but I can. You the same as anybody else."

"If I ever lie down for a man the first time I see him I'll go the whole hog and charge him for it. That would keep both of us honest, at least."

"Do me a favor," said Benteen. "Go over and help Charlie cook supper. Anything. Don't just sit here."

"The hell with you," she said.

Range work soon wiped out all other worries. The intermittent snow continued, the temperature sometimes dropped to forty below at night, abating but little during the days. It created an entirely new set of conditions for the outfit to face.

Along with his Texans, Benteen had learned many a wintering trick from the Montana nesters. Snow blindness was a constant threat, and this they tried to ward off either by smearing the skin about their eyes with charcoal or by cutting the black lining out of their coats and making masks. "I got her once," Fadiman said. "It's like having needles in your eyes. Spent the miserablest week of my life, flat on my back with salt poultices on my eyes."

Another trick was to carry pine splinters soaked in coal oil. A man never knew when he might be set down somewhere on the lethal prairie, and the splinters would quickly catch fire from a match and build on into a campfire. The riders had to dress with the thought of surviving some lonely, bitter night. They doubled or tripled every item of clothing and hunted around for more.

Before putting on their two pairs of wool socks, they chilled their feet in the snow then dried them with brisk rubbing. When they had pulled on their boots they splashed warm water over them, and an airtight sheath of ice formed quickly. The result, Benteen found, was feet twice as warm as a man dared expect.

They wore mittens over gloves, wrapped their heads and often tied down the brims of their hats to protect their ears. They pulled chaps over overalls and wool pants. They warmed the bits of their bridles before asking the horses to take them into tender mouths. They had frostbitten fingers, feet and cheeks and had to rub them alive again with coal oil. They cursed Montana, swore it was hell with the heat turned off.

None of that was quite enough. The cold crept through everything. It numbed the brain, slashed heaving lungs, poured out again as white vapor.

It began to kill.

There was by then an average depth of two feet of snow. In places it was five times that deep, and there remained fewer and fewer stretches where grass lay exposed to the cattle. They ate sage tops and chewed the willows and cottonwoods, floundered into drifts or slid into air holes in frozen streams. The punchers began to find carcasses. What remained standing didn't much look like range cattle.

"It's sure sickenin'," Mel Kinder said once, "to see big fours and fives wobbling along like new calves."

But the bluffs helped Bitter Creek. That was made clear to Benteen each time he bucked his horse through the drifts to the Sage Creek line camp. The throughs being wintered there were going fast. Right out of Texas, they had built no resistance to a northern winter. He had to undertake the heartbreaking job of bringing them across through the Bar D gap and shifting hardier stock to Sage Creek. The horses' feet were always bleeding, while the cattle had the hair and hide worn from their legs to the hocks.

They were soon senseless brutes, resigned, no longer rustling for themselves. They sought only shelter and finding it, however feeble, would stand until they dropped. Through some ancient instinct, Shannon's cattle, drifted to the northern bluffs by the scouring wind, tried to get through to the more sheltered south slope. They began to pile up on the fences the stockman had built. Benteen saw that without any sense of satisfaction. The work of a two-edged sword, however justified, was not good to see.

Day after day Bitter Creek mounted weakened horses and bucked its way through the snow. The riders had to pull steers out of the drifts. They had to haze the hungry to some place where there was more to eat. They had to break ice from the waterholes over and over, a job that kept two riders busy constantly.

They no longer bothered to count the carcasses.

Benteen, whenever it was clear enough to see out across the prairie, had a hollow feeling all through him. He knew by then that the same bitter conditions prevailed all over Montana and Wyoming, western Dakota and western Nebraska and western Kansas. The northern plains had come to disaster, a big disaster men would speak of with hushed breaths. It would be a year to remember, a year of fury, of natural horror.

And disaster had come to Sage Creek a little more than it had touched Bitter Creek.

Sometimes from a high point Benteen watched Slash S riders fight their own battle. Shannon no longer had time to think of his enemies—he was fighting to save his own. Benteen had seen a sample of what the Sage Creek outfits were experiencing in what had happened to his own throughs, what kept right on happening to the hardier steers he had moved to the upper Sage.

Wind off the Canadian prairies screamed unbroken across the Missouri slope. It was a tremendous pressure upon the cattle, pushing them south, ever south. What it touched it blighted, and what it blighted it soon killed.

Regardless of their owners, he had pity for the steers.

He talked more and more to Linda, to Fadiman or whoever else would listen, of the change that had to

come to the range. Men had no moral right to specu-
late with the lives of so many millions of animals, turning them loose to fight for their existence and yet to
make fortunes for their proprietors. A man ought not
to own a head of stock he could not take care of prop-
erly. Benteen swore he never would again.

Riding south of Bar D one day he encountered Wad
Dennis on the range.

"How you doin'?" Benteen asked quietly.

Wad made a restless, circling motion with his hand.
"Same as you. A man's not doin' any good out fightin'
this stuff. But he rides out and fights it. You move a
steer here, then you move him there, hopin' it'll help.
But it don't."

"Only helps the man doin' the ridin', I guess," Benteen admitted. "And him not much. How're the Mead-
owses?"

Wad looked up from the snow in bleak earnestness.
"Kids come back quick. They got bounce. But Edith—
Man, every time I see that smashed look in her eyes I
want to gut-shoot the bastard that done it to her."

"I reckon you're doin' her more good the way it is,
Wad."

The wind died that night; there was no snow. But
the piercing cold cut through the buildings, nullified
the fires in the stoves, crept into bed when a man tried
to sleep. Benteen turned restlessly. By the calendar the
winter was just really starting. Less than a week remained of January, but there was no reason to hope
that February and March would be any better. What
Wad had said that day kept coming back. Nothing a
man tried actually did any good. Maybe it only weakened the steers so that it would be kinder to leave them
to die quickly. It ought to be easier to freeze than
slowly to starve. Either ought to be easier than to have
to watch it happen.

He was having breakfast ahead of the crew the next
morning when Eph Fadiman rode in. The man's horse

showed how hard he had driven it. Benteen sprang to the door as Fadiman swung out of the saddle.

"Eph, what's wrong?" Benteen asked.

Fadiman came up the steps and lurched on into the room. "There's Slash S steers on my place."

"How come?"

"Shannon ripped out his goddam fences, that's how come. The one above me I seen, and it's ten to one he done the same to the rest. He's dumped his stuff on top of us, Benteen."

Benteen stood in stunned silence while the nester moved mechanically to the stove, stripped off mittens and gloves and began to warm his hands carefully, rubbing them, not holding them too close. Riders began to arrive from the bunkhouse. They seated themselves at the table, aware of the tight silence of Benteen, wondering about it but asking no questions.

When the crew had eaten breakfast, Benteen issued terse orders: "Mel, you and Kit check the Shannon fences west of the Bar D gap. You keep on choppin' ice, Harry. Me and Eph will check the east sections of the bluffs. It's probable the gaps are all open. Shannon really needs Bitter Creek now to survive. So he's set out to take it by force."

"What do we do with the Slash S stuff we see?" Mel asked. "Shoot it?"

"The steers never started this war, boys. Just the same we don't have grass or browse to carry our own stuff. Try to haze the Slash S's back if you can and close the gaps."

Dressed cumbersomely, as was his regular practice now, Benteen rode out with Fadiman. As they neared the divide on the nester's range, he began to see Slash S cattle. They were all clinging to the bluffs, using their shelter. The two men rode on to the gap Fadiman had inspected earlier. The barbed wire was laid back, the strands cut by cutters.

It was the same on east, at three other gaps.

The two horsemen were riding slowly back when

Benteen saw in the far distance a party of several riders.

"Somebody from the other side!" Fadiman said urgently. "They come through the gap and seen our tracks! They're followin' 'em!"

"You're right," Benteen agreed.

They rode on unhesitantly, but with their eyes glued to the enlarging shapes. "One's Con, sure as hell," Fadiman said quietly, and Benteen nodded. His gun was under his coat because he had not expected an encounter like this. He unfastened the two lower buttons so he could lift the edge of the coat and get at the gun's cold grips.

Shannon had a look of satisfaction on his face as the two parties came together. The six men with him were all strangers to Benteen, who noticed Fadiman eyeing them puzzledly, also.

"It's too much to expect that you'd be pickin' up your strays," Fadiman said bitterly.

"Just aimed to tell you," Shannon answered, "to leave them fences alone. They're on my land. And leave my steers alone."

"*They're* on our land," Fadiman retorted.

"You're wrong there. You have always been trespassers. Which is somethin' I don't aim to tolerate no more."

Fadiman's mouth had opened, his breath steamed out. "Just takin' the south slope over, huh?"

"Takin' it back," Shannon corrected.

Benteen could hear his own teeth grating, felt the tension in his jaws. He said, "If you only wanted to use this side of the bluffs for shelter, Shannon, we wouldn't say anything. Your critters are sufferin' worse than ours. But let 'em stray onto our graze and you'll have trouble. Too bad it's got to be that way, but you called the dance yourself."

Shannon's eyes held an odd glitter. He started to speak, reconsidered, and only nodded to his men. They rode on east.

"The pure gall of him," Fadiman exploded. "And I wonder why he's picked up them extra punchers?"

"Know 'em?" asked Benteen.

"A couple. But they usually ride for a Musselshell outfit. Nick, that Shannon's set himself for a finish fight, and it's startin' already. He's sent to Miles City and the other winterin' towns for the men he'll need."

"Sure looks like it."

"What we gonna do?"

"Eph, I sure wish I knew."

They continued west through the impeding snow. The air was still clear, the temperature somewhere below zero. It had a cutting edge in Benteen's lungs and seemed even to enter his stomach.

They met Mel and Kit an hour later. All the gaps were open, and there was more. "They got a war party over on this side to see we don't close 'em again," Mel reported. "We run spang into 'em."

Benteen and Fadiman exchanged bleak glances.

"That cinches it," Fadiman said, "and they're over here for more than to keep the gaps open. They're gonna let their steers eat and throw ours into the drifts to freeze. That'll make us fight, then they'll butcher us. You wait and see."

"How many men did you see, Mel?" Benteen asked.

"Five, all tough. Never seen 'em on the roundup."

Fadiman groaned. "I was right. With his own outfit, he's got twice what we could handle. Shannon never figured on meetin' us. He was just over here to show them gun hands the lay of the land and point out what they should do."

"You seen Shannon and didn't shoot him?" Kit gasped.

Benteen's eyes withered him silent.

Fadiman returned home, while Benteen rode back to Bar D with his men. For the first time since he had come to Montana, Benteen felt beaten. Fadiman had pointed out nothing he had not seen for himself. Short of a miracle, there was nothing to prevent this ugly winter from handing Bitter Creek to Shannon, after all.

Or short of open, ruinous fighting.

Benteen fought the temptation of that alternate course. Given nobody but his own men, he would have started already. But the nesters were married, except for Damon who meant to marry soon. They could not stand up against a force three times their size without being cut to pieces. Yet, if he knew the nesters, nothing this side of hell could hold them back.

Never in his life had Benteen used his gun deliberately on another man, but he had to now. The fury that had ruled his life, since that long ago day on the Kansas prairie, began to center on that realization. Shannon was scum, worse than many who had faced the ruinous roar of his gun. *If I'd done it sooner, Meadows would be alive,* Benteen thought.

His mind settled firm on the decision. It was not fear that ruled out the thought of penetrating the rattlesnake den of Slash S and simply crowding the man until he fought. A sense of decency made it necessary that he have honor with him in the showdown. Shannon was moving into Bitter Creek, and the next time he appeared he would not leave it alive.

CHAPTER SIXTEEN

No effort was made that day to move the Slash S invaders out of the shelter of the bluffs and onto Bitter Creek's exposed nourishment. The nesters and Bar D riders kept a close watch, and if an attempt had been made it would have brought on a quick and bitter fight. Shannon was moving slowly, with extreme care. He was playing for keeps.

Benteen was roused out of sleep that night by a loud rapping on the bunkhouse door. He pulled on his trousers, and when he opened the door to the freezing inrush of air, Linda stood there on the steps.

"Cassie's at the house! There's been trouble!"

"What?"

"She wouldn't say. She wants to see you."

"Be over in a minute. And you get out of that wind."

Benteen had a sick feeling when he looked at Kit's bunk and saw that it was empty. Dressing hurriedly, he remembered that this was the first clear night in a long while. He knew where Kit had gone, a little of what the trouble had been, already.

Cassie was in Linda's kitchen, blown by the wind, looking frozen, almost dead. Linda had built up the fire, was making coffee. Cassie stared at Benteen and opened her mouth. She tried to speak twice before the words came out.

"Kit Beckner—Scarfield—shot him."

"I knew it already," Benteen whispered.

"I didn't encourage him—you've got to believe that! Tonight Scarfield was there—and Kit came."

"He's dead?"

"No. That's why I came here—you've got to get a doctor."

"Your father send you instead of makin' the ride himself?"

Bitterly she said, "Ira is afraid of you people. Scared to death."

"Get some hot coffee in her, Linda," Benteen said as he wheeled toward the door.

He roused Mel Kinder and told him to head for town and bring the doctor. He got into his outer clothing and saddled a horse, which he led to where Cassie's stood in front of the house. When he stepped back into the kitchen, Linda was forcing coffee down Cassie.

"I got to go back with her," he said.

Linda nodded.

There was nothing left of the coquette in Cassie now, Benteen thought, riding with her toward the Glade ranch, west of Bar D. The night held a piercing coldness, yet the air was almost still. The moon was out, beyond it and all about was the hot-seeming brilliance of stars.

"Scarfield still there?" Benteen asked, his voice begging her to say that he was.

"He cleared out."

Their horses plowed on. So old was the packed snow, so solidly settled, that it held up well. Cassie knew the way better than he, and at her lead they came finally across the top-of-land and were moving down to the little nester setup by the frozen prairie lake. The leaves were gone from the few trees now; they looked like witches' brooms stuck upright in the snow. There was a light in the house.

Ira Glade was seated by the fire when Benteen stepped into the house with Cassie. He didn't look up, yet Benteen saw his whole body tighten. He said nothing, nor did Benteen. Cassie led the way through a curtain into an adjoining bedroom. Kit was conscious. His eyes were open and moved toward Benteen, glazed with pain. Cassie or somebody had got his shirt off. There was an edge of crude bandage showing at the end of the quilts.

Benteen walked to the bed and turned the covers back a little. The bandage covered the outside of Kit's right shoulder and stretched across his chest.

"So you finally got too big for your britches," Benteen said.

Cassie had stepped out of the room. Kit wet his lips. He said, "It was Glade I tried to kill."

"What's that?"

"That scurvy, low-lifed animal—Glade. They know, and it won't hurt 'em to hear again. When I rode in tonight, I seen Scarfield's horse at the porch. I figured it was time we knew what was goin' on here. I left my cayuse and sneaked in. Got under the window where I could hear. Glade was tyin' into Cassie. Orderin' her to get in bed with Scarfield. Either tryin' to save his measly spread from Shannon or his miserable life. I come in and tried to kill the bastard. Scarfield stopped me. That's all. Except for one thing. You've all roweled me hard about wantin' to have her, myself. It ain't that. I loved her the minute I seen her. All I want's to help her out. That's why I went crazy when I heard Glade order her to—

"Kit," said Benteen, "I apologize for me and the boys. Mel's gone for the doctor. How bad're you hit?"

"Got a busted shoulder."

"Just take it easy. I want a little powwow with Ira, myself."

Glade was still in his chair. Cassie stood across the room, her back turned, staring out the window.

"What's your outfit worth, Glade?" Benteen said.

Glade tried to bring belligerence into his face, but there was only a slack grayness.

Cassie whirled. "The price of my sleeping with Scarfield. Whatever value he puts on that."

Benteen shot his gaze at her. "Know what Shannon would have paid him, back before he decided to take everything by force?"

"Five thousand."

"Five thousand's it. Write out a bill of sale, Glade. You're travelin'. Tonight."

"Now, you look here!" Glade shouted. "That girl's a bitch, and there's no use gettin' on your high horse about her. And what makes you think you could hold this spread, even if I sold it to you? Shannon's takin' the works. He's got the men to do it. And more. He don't figure on takin' sass, and Scarfield's gonna tend to them that give it. He said so tonight. Just laughed when I offered to sell. He wanted Cassie."

"So," said Cassie, "my devoted father was going over to Bullnose's for the night, leaving me to buy his immunity."

"Get him writin' materials."

Cassie got them, put them on the table by the lamp. Glade sat hunched in his chair. But he was thinking. Presently he got up and walked to the table. He sat down and began to write. He threw down the pen in a gust of temper and stood up.

Benteen got his checkbook from his coat pocket and took the same chair. He wrote two checks, one of which he gave to Glade. The sullen man stared at it, his face turning bitterly suspicious.

"You said five thousand. This is for twenty-five hundred."

"So's the other one. It's made out to Cassie."

"Now, look here!"

"It'll take about fifteen minutes for you to saddle a horse and get ridin', Glade. I wouldn't be around here any longer. Or ever show up in this country again."

Benteen examined the bill of sale. It was made out right, five hundred head of steers book count, three hundred and twenty acres of land with buildings. He kept staring at it until he heard the outside door close. When he looked up there were only himself and Cassie in the room. A little later he saw Glade ride out in the moonlight. Maybe he was going to Slash S to throw in openly with the other side. Maybe he was quitting the country while he could. Benteen didn't really care.

"That deal all right?" he asked Cassie.

She only nodded her head.

When he looked in on Kit, the kid seemed to be asleep. Benteen went back to the other room, rolled a cigarette.

"Nobody ever felt that way about me before," Cassie said, very softly, nodding toward the bedroom. "Not wanting anything from me. But ready to die for me. Not even you. Nick, I'm not the bitch Ira called me. I acted that way, but—" She broke off.

"Maybe we haven't understood you. Any more than we understood Kit."

"He's a fine boy. No—man. Do you want me to leave, too?" Cassie nodded toward the check in her name, which still lay on the table.

"Not if you don't want to."

"I don't. And I won't—give you any trouble."

"Think Scarfield'll be back?"

Cassie nodded. "He's bound to be. Wheedling and flattery didn't get him what he wanted. Extortion didn't. There's still force."

"You willin' to help me try to trap him here?"

Promptly she said, "I'll do anything *you* want, Nick. You know that already."

"He won't wait long. The first time he thinks you're alone—"

"He'll come."

"And I'll be here, not you."

Mel Kinder could not reach Yellow Bluff and return with the doctor before noon the next day. For that reason, Benteen was relieved when, an hour later, Charlie and Chunk—both of whom had been fond of Kit in spite of their bantering—came in, unable to endure the suspense of not knowing fully what had happened to him. They arrived in the jumper sleigh, prepared to haul a man or a body back to Bar D.

"Fine," Benteen greeted them. "He's some shot up but likely not in much danger. You boys take him and Cassie home."

"What you gonna do?" Charlie asked suspiciously.

"I bought Glade out. Reckon I'll stay and look the place over in the morning."

They didn't believe him but said no more.

They made the sleigh ready, straw in the bed, blankets over that. They placed a well-wrapped Kit on this pallet. Then Benteen asked Cassie to get in with him, lying beside Kit and covered up. There was a chance that Scarfield was watching the house even now. Benteen got his own horse and rode out with the sleigh across the height of land.

There he dismounted and, tying the horse to the back of the sleigh, turned back afoot. He moved slowly, carefully, keeping to the bottom of a hollow until he came in behind Glade's barn. He was soon back in the house, alone, and waiting for Dike Scarfield.

He knew it might take a long and wearing time. Scarfield had been forced to clear out when Cassie announced her intention of getting help for Kit. Maybe he had gone to wherever he was holing up, or possibly he had only moved out to keep watch on the house. If so, he had seen Glade leaving. And Benteen was sure he had not let himself be seen when he worked back in.

He sat in darkness, not even permitting himself the comfort of smoking for fear his man might be trying to spy through a window. He had done his best to build up the picture of everyone but Cassie leaving here. That was his bait.

He began to ache in his motionless tension. He could hear the timbers of the house groan and creak in the cold but dared not add fuel to the dying fire for fear of sparks that would warn of somebody's stirring. Then, because the chilled air carried sound so loudly, he was warned of a stirring in the ranchyard.

He prowled on silent feet to the window's side. A

figure had ridden slowly around the upper end of the little lake and come in between the house and barn. He thought it was the bundled shape of Glade, returning now that Cassie was alone to force her to endorse the other check over to him. Then the horse was closer, and the figure was too big for Glade.

He could have killed the man then and there, as once before he could have shot him in the back, but he waited. The rider swung out of the saddle, turned and came nearer—Scarfield. He was cut from sight as he came onto the porch. He tried the door, which Benteen had thought to lock as Cassie would if alone. Scarfield was careful to make little noise. For a moment he stood outside the door separating him from what he wanted.

Then Scarfield's shoulder hit the door hard, three times, and it burst inward. He stepped into the room and shut the door. He stood waiting, perhaps suspicious because there had been no outcry, wondering if Cassie had slept through the noise.

Crouched behind the stove, Benteen held his breath. He heard something drop to the floor and realized it was Scarfield's heavy coat. The man was getting ready. Benteen could picture his excitement as he anticipated his conquest. Then Scarfield was walking very slowly across the room toward the curtain of Cassie's bedroom.

A moment later, as he realized the emptiness of her bed, he cursed.

He came back more noisily, brushing aside the curtain, stepping out. Benteen was standing up then. Scarfield turned his head and saw him.

The man's breath gushed out.

Dimly, through the room's faint illumination, Benteen saw that stabbing hand. His own slid into action. They seemed to fire together. He heard the rip of lead through the stovepipe beside him. He saw the curtain swaying. Scarfield had cut back into the bedroom.

There was a window in there. The man could crash through it in hope of escape. Benteen stood tense and motionless, listening hard. But Scarfield realized he could not get away. By the time he could be on his feet, Benteen would be on the porch, outside and after him. This was final. Scarfield wasn't getting paid for it, but this time he could not run.

"That's you, ain't it, Benteen?"

"It's not Cassie, damn you. Why don't you go through the window?" Benteen taunted. "Nobody here to see your yellow stripe but me. I already know about it. Man enough to buy or rape a woman, but that's all."

Scarfield burst back into the room; he came with a blazing gun. Benteen danced out from behind the stove, crouched, his gun up and kicking its constant jar to his shoulder socket. Lead splintered the window, tore through the side of his shirt. It stopped coming. When Benteen's finger froze on the trigger, the smoky room was silent.

For a second—until the jar when Scarfield fell.

Benteen walked over very slowly, the wrath and violence spent. This was a treacherous thing on the floor ahead of him, perhaps still a living thing. But it wasn't. Dike Scarfield was dead.

The feeling began to come back, then, the sickness in every flesh cell, the dying violence in every brain cell. He was only half aware of kicking Scarfield's loosened gun to the far end of the room, hearing it crash there against the wall. A shudder went through him.

CHAPTER SEVENTEEN

It was snowing hard when Benteen reached Bar D on a Glade horse just after daybreak. It seemed to him that the temperature had fallen ten degrees during the ride over. The sky was an ugly black; he had seen nothing like it all winter. Charlie was standing in the chuckhouse doorway, Arno in that of the bunkhouse and, at the ranch house, Linda held a door against the shoving wind, looking uncertainly through the curtain of snow toward him.

"It's over," he called to the men. "Scarfield didn't make it. Come take this cayuse, Harry. I'm froze."

He swung out of saddle and left the horse for Arno to pick up and take care of. Tramping through the snow he moved toward the house. Linda didn't speak until she had closed the door behind him.

She said, "It's been a hundred years since you left here."

"Where's Kit?"

"In my father's old bed. Cassie's in mine, sleeping finally. Nick, are you all right?"

He made himself grin. "So damned all right, I'm starved. Fix me some breakfast." He wanted casualness, routine things, lightness. He had never liked to kill a man; he would never develop the appetite in the way of a Scarfield.

"This snow," Linda said as she got busy at the stove. "I'm worried about Mel and the doctor. They might have to turn in somewhere before they get here."

"It's sure thick."

"An hour or two, and we won't be able to see the barn. Nick, the boys had better string up ropes to help find their way around. I mean it."

He grinned again, making his muscles form the smile. "You don't get to do much bossin' on Bar D. So that's a order, and I'll sure carry it out." He had started to get out of his coat, but he buttoned it again.

Crossing to the bunkhouse, he told Arno he thought they were in for their first real ground blizzard. He wanted headquarters made ready, and no one was to leave until the thing ended or blew over. He was worried about the steers, the boys at the line camp, Mel and the doctor. There was one small comfort. Shannon and the huge fighting force he had gathered would be pinned down, too. It would be a breathing spell.

Linda had bacon, potatoes and coffee on the table by the time he got back. Ordinarily he would have eaten in Charlie's kitchen, but he had sensed the intense strain in her, knew she had to get moving along accustomed lines herself.

She didn't refer directly to Scarfield, instead saying, "Cassie feels responsible for what happened to Kit. She wants to take care of him. I had trouble getting her to rest."

Benteen looked up from his eating. "She experienced somethin' she never did before, at least in a long while. A man's givin' instead of takin' away. I think it got through to her. Mebbe there'll be somethin' there, Linda. I sure hope there is."

She was frowning as she stared at him. Then, "If there is, you'll be between them. She'll be between you —and me. Nick, why did you have to do it?"

"Some day you'll know."

She had taken the lift out of the moment. She moved off into the other room, maybe to check on Kit—or to get away.

Mel and the doctor wallowed in through the steadily mounting storm around two that afternoon. Doc Fisher proved to be a stocky man when he emerged from his wolfskin cap and buffalo coat. He wore steel-rimmed glasses, which fogged promptly and heavily in the indoor warmth.

When he had his fingers working again, he went in to Kit. Benteen helped him. There wasn't much to do. Fisher found that Scarfield's bullet had smashed the shoulder bone then deflected upward, emerging. Disinfectant, a splint and tight bandages, and Kit figured he was ready to be up and about.

"Not much," Fisher told him flatly. "Not for three or four days, at least. Hell, man, you've got two pretty girls to nurse you. I'd trade places."

When they had emerged into the kitchen for the coffee Linda had ready for Fisher, Benteen looked at the doctor.

"Mebbe you can't trade places with him, but you're gonna have a vacation. You can't go back to town in this."

"Man, I've got patients—" Fisher looked out the window and scowled. "Looks like you're right till tomorrow, anyhow."

"If then," said Benteen.

At dark the ranch thermometer stood at sixty three below zero, and the wind was a streaming mass of snow, more lifted from the ground than falling from the lost sky. The reading of the mercury column was itself a shock, but actually, in this first day of being snowbound, there was an odd release, almost a festivity in the men.

Through no fault of their own they had been relieved temporarily of the terrible responsibility of the cattle, the eternal hostility of Shannon—and even the doctor did not seem greatly to mind his temporary imprisonment. Bar D's commissary was full, its woodpile high, its buildings soundly constructed.

When Benteen groped his way to the cook house for supper, he was struck by the flushness of Charlie's face. He thought little of it, for the meal was on time, up to its usual standard. Yet he lingered afterward, and to his surprise Charlie came over to the closest seat and settled his great weight wearily. His head rocked forward onto his arms, and Benteen shot to his feet.

When he put his hand on the back of Charlie's neck, he lifted it quickly.

"You're on fire! What's the matter?"

"Nothin' much," Charlie said, looking up through glazed eyes. "My feet hurt. Thought I'd set a minute."

"You're sick."

"Well," said Charlie, "I went out to the woodpile this afternoon. In my shirt sleeves, and I was kinda warm from the stove, I guess. Never realized it was so cold out there." His teeth began to chatter as if from the thought of it.

Benteen was on his way to get Fisher, whom Linda had asked to stay at the house. She rushed over with him. The doctor took Charlie's temperature, peeled back his eyes and looked at them.

"Bed for you," he said.

"Yeah," Charlie agreed. "Be all right in the morning."

"Not here," Linda said promptly. "Too noisy, and you won't be all right in the morning. You're moving over to the house."

Charlie glared at her. "Who's gonna cook?"

"I am."

Charlie didn't like it. His face twisted in protest. Benteen grinned at him, hiding his deep worry. "You're a sly old fox. A pill-shooter on hand and two purty nurses. How come I let you beat me to that idea?"

Charlie had started shaking. His head rolled. Benteen got blankets off the bed in the kitchen and threw them around the cook. He and the doctor got him over to the house. Linda ordered him into her bed.

"I'll take his," she decided. "Cassie can nurse and sleep on the couch. Doc, I'm afraid you'll have to go to the bunkhouse with the boys."

Benteen knew she wanted it to be that way. She wasn't easy being in the same house with Cassie, no matter what good friends they might once have been. Cassie was an eternal reminder of a thing she hated.

Cassie proved herself a good nurse. They got the old cook into bed and covered up. They put heated bricks in with him, and Fisher gave him something to swallow.

The feeling of festivity was gone.

Benteen helped Linda move over to the cook house, taking back the blankets, making up the bed in Charlie's kitchen again.

"Sure you want to do this?" he asked. "Lot of the boys are good cooks. They'll be scrappin' purty soon, nothin' to do."

"Of course I want to do it."

"It'll ·get damned cold here in the middle of the night if you don't keep the fire up."

"Get's damned cold at the house at night if you don't, too."

Irritation was all through her now, partly nerves, partly deeper emotions. He left before he made it worse.

The sky was shut off. The ground blizzard rolled across Bar D so that window light did not show from one building to another. Benteen used the rope leading to the bunkhouse, as if it were a sidewalk in a town, hearing the high scream of the wind. He didn't want to look at the thermometer again. Sixty below was cold enough. Below fifty things died quickly, their lungs frosted, while trees exploded with the crack of rifle shots.

Every man in the bunkhouse that night slept restlessly. Three times Benteen got up and refueled the stove, each time dressing, finding his way to the cook house and stoking both the heater and the kitchen range. If Linda awakened, she gave no sign of it. He could see her faintly by the flickering light from the stove draft. Her hair was in two braids, and she looked like a very small girl asleep.

There was no letup at morning, although dawn was only a dirty grayness that crept into the atmosphere.

The well was frozen so solid no amount of hot water would thaw it, but there were plenty of hands to melt snow. Men broke their way to the barn, following the guide rope, to take care of the horses, which now had to satisfy their thirst by licking snow.

Linda had breakfast ready on time, and it was a good one. Afterward, over her objections, Benteen put Arno to washing the dishes. She said, "Then I'd better go over and let Cassie get some sleep."

"There's plenty of boys to spell her," Benteen said, and saw she was relieved.

But he went to the house with the doctor. Kit was in good shape, fretting to get up. Charlie was not in good shape, although he wanted to get up, too. But his temperature was down a little.

"You missed pneumonia, if you've missed it," said Fisher, "by the skin of your teeth."

"If I'd thought to taken a couple of drinks—and if I'd had 'em on hand to take—"

"Or if you'd had a few more inches of tallow on you," gibed Benteen.

Charlie said something under his breath. He was holding his own if not getting better.

This day was a slow grind, in which nerves tightened and tempers were honed to a fine edge. That night a fight started in the bunkhouse between Arno and Mel, the oldest of friends, over some trivial point in a card game. The men came to their feet simultaneously, the table went over, the lamp spilling with a crash. That ended it, for they all jumped on the burning coal oil. Benteen made them shake hands. Privately he felt like banging their heads together just for the pleasure of banging them.

The storm continued without abatement through that night, through another—and the third—day. During that day steers drifted blindly through headquarters and vanished into the ground blizzard again.

They're moving, Benteen thought. *Everything moving—or gone.*

After supper that evening he stayed at the cook house, knowing what it was like to be there alone, growing alarmed at Linda's stubborn hostility against Cassie— and growing annoyed. She refused to play cards with him or to talk beyond answering his questions as briefly as possible, making some vague reply to his statements or none at all.

At last he said, "Damn it, Linda, come over to the bunkhouse and listen to the boys yarnin'. That's better than settin' here brooding."

She looked at him in bright anger. "Who's brooding?"

"You are. Sulking like a just-weaned calf."

She was out of Charlie's rocker and on her feet instantly.

"I'd rather be an unweaned calf than a human bull—"

He got up and caught the wrists of her clenched hands. She tried to break them free.

"Or a bitch in heat," she taunted.

It was the storm, that was all, magnifying by at least ten times her former resentment. Her hurt—her jealousy. He tried to remember that as he held onto her hands, not so much to still them as to keep his own from striking out. Storm, too—they were crazy with it, fear and concern bursting out of them through their weaknesses, his guilt and her unforgivingness.

"Get out of here," she said in a dull voice at last. "And stay away. You can eat at the house. You'd like it better, anyhow."

He flung down her hands and walked out.

When he reached the bunkhouse, there was what should be good news. The temperature was climbing a little, Mel reported, was up nearly ten points. "Long ways to go, though, to get outta that hole," the puncher commented. "And what're we gonna find when we can get out on the range?"

It was a question nobody wanted to answer. It didn't have to be answered. They knew before it had been asked.

Yet there was an easing from the mere fact that it had grown a little warmer. Charlie was better, Kit stewing in his young juice. Benteen began to calm down. But the scene in the cook house remained vivid, immediate.

The temperature was still at fifty below. He was aware of that when he awakened some time in the night. Relaxing nerves had let the men sleep better, himself included. Nobody had been up to put more wood in the stove. He got out of bed and attended to it. He hesitated a moment before he dressed and made his way over to the cook house.

His coming in didn't awaken Linda. He refueled both the stoves very quietly. When he was finished, he crept slowly, silently to the side of her bed. Her face was relaxed in the dimmest of light, she seemed to be smiling. The last of his anger oozed out of him, and he smiled down at that little creasing of contentment on her mouth. He dropped to his knees and very gently kissed the smile.

Her eyes came open. He felt the quick little side-jerk of her head. Then it quit moving, his mouth still on the edge of hers.

"Nick," she whispered, "I'm sorry."

He wasn't quite sure of everything he did after that.

The dream quality did not fade until they were lying in each other's arms, breathing easily. Then he was completely aware of everything. "I never intended—" he began.

"I love you—"

"You got to believe me—"

"I don't care. I wanted it to happen. Thank God it did."

She knew now, she belonged to life—and to him.

CHAPTER EIGHTEEN

THE DRIFT WAS ON. Morning came clear, though ridden by the wind from the north, a magnetic repulsion from the pole, shoving everything ahead of it. Bar D was a speck in a sea of drift. Cattle came out of Canada to cross the border; they moved on the northern Missouri slope to the river and its ice where they slid into air holes or fell on the ice to freeze helplessly; they staggered half dead across Sage Creek and the bluffs and Bitter Creek; they bogged belly-deep in drifts and froze upright.

There was nothing to eat.

There was nothing to drink.

Nothing could be done about it.

Men tried. Benteen was in the saddle in the first dirty light. He saw brands wholly strange to him burned starkly on the loose hides of stumbling bones. As day strengthened to a glaring white hell, he pushed his horse against the snow and made his way to Fadiman's.

"Nothin' short of the south pole'll stop 'em," the nester said in spent bitterness. "It's all gone. Sage Creek, Bitter Creek, the whole damned cow country. When they get the drift in 'em, they're goin', that's all."

"If the wind'd die—"

"If the chinook'd blow. It won't. Not for weeks, months—never again, mebbe. We'll go into eternity froze up. Ice statues—all of us. Froze tighter'n a bull's rear end in fly time. But, by God, Con Shannon—he's wiped out, too."

Benteen said, "The range is still here, Eph."

"I faintly remember. Belly-deep in snow."

Furiously, Benteen said, "There's still steers in Texas and Oregon and Washington. There's horses and saddles and punchers. All it takes, by God."

"Except for somethin' I ain't got. Money. Mebbe I can keep the family alive till spring on the beef money. That's all I can hope for now."

"Eph, we got to do something. Get to the Yellowstone and try to hold the stuff there in the valley and the breaks. Keep it from crossin'. Bring as much as we can through."

Fadiman laughed. It wasn't pleasant to hear, that laughter of a man who could not cry. "If that's ten per cent—well, I'll eat anything over that."

"I'm gonna make up the Meadows sleigh for a chuckwagon again," Benteen retorted. "I'm takin' my boys and ridin' the river. You others want to come along or stay home and bellyache?"

The nester was staring at him. "You just don't quit, do you." It wasn't a question.

"Not till I'm licked."

"If you ain't now, you'll never be. Benteen, if you think it'll do any good to ride the river, I'll ride it with you. So'll the others."

"It'll do good if it only keeps us busy."

"When'll you be ready?"

"Tomorrow mornin'," Benteen said.

Returned to Bar D he told Linda what he meant to do. She agreed promptly to the undertaking, punishing though it would be to the men involved. Charlie wanted to go, so did Kit, but neither was in shape for it. Benteen sent Mel to the Meadows place to bring the big sleigh. He bucked his way to the Sage Creek line camp.

There wasn't a Bitter Creek steer to be found over there; they had all gone south in the drift.

"Seen somethin' funny last night," Friday said. "Not long after midnight. Big outfit cut around here, headin' south. I happened to be up. There was enough moonlight so I was sure I made out Shannon. They passed up the Bar D gap and went through the next one, from the tracks I seen this mornin'."

"Kept out of our gap so we wouldn't notice the tracks," Benteen mused. "That means a sneak play, Burt. Wonder what the hell they're up to now."

"Leavin' on the sly that way," Friday said, "they wanted an early start at whatever it is."

"All horsebackers? No sleds?"

"Just riders. But a couple of dozen. That's what made me so curious."

Benteen told the two line riders to move back to headquarters and get ready for the river riding. He plowed on through virgin snow to the next gap west. There he saw the scuffed trail of the horseback party, coming from the north, going through to the south side of the bluffs. He followed. They passed the Glade house, where Scarfield still lay frozen, without stopping. The party could have found better going but had chosen to hammer its way through unbroken snow.

He followed until he was abreast of Edith Meadows's place, then turned in. Wad had seen him coming, was waiting outside. He had the same beaten look Fadiman had worn. Benteen told him of the new undertaking, of the trail he had followed out of Sage Basin.

"That's what Shannon's gonna do," Wad reflected. "Ride the river."

"I reckon," Benteen agreed. "And it worries me their pullin' out in the middle of the night to get on it. He's got somethin' up his sleeve sure as hell."

He saw Mel Kinder coming in with a team. He and Wad helped get the horses hitched to the heavy-duty sleigh, and Benteen rode back to Bar D with Mel. They soon had the chuck box bolted on and began stocking it with supplies. Over in the bunkhouse a couple of men were making up bedrolls, using plenty of blankets. They had learned much on the frozen drive to Dakota.

By night they were ready to go, Benteen fighting down his deviling sense of urgency, forcing himself to the patient thoroughness with which he had planned the drive before. The saddle band was made up again, of only the strongest horses. Bedding, clothing, food— he prepared for a long ordeal.

The nesters appeared in the evening to be ready for an early start—Damon, Fadiman, Hollister, Smithwick and the rest—all except Bullnose Wells. They were quiet, their hope burning only in a flicker but living still on the flimsy basis of the untested plan. Men of their kind could not be defeated even though they were destroyed.

The next morning, leaving the nesters to bring on cavvy and sleigh, Benteen rode forward with Dennis, Kinder, Cooper, Arno and Friday, a restless need in him to determine why Slash S had stolen off in the night, im- mediately after it became apparent that the ground blizzard had quieted down. Two miles south of the Meadows's spread they came to the place where the Shannon riders had cut back to the main road to Yellow Bluff and proceeded steadily southward toward the Yellowstone. A little later the party left this road, cut- ting a due southward course, straight down the wind.

The horses stumbled across the snow, not sinking in the deep, helpless way of the cattle, yet heavily impeded. Benteen realized it would take them all that day to reach the river. He began to feel the futility of the work they could do there, trying to fend the cattle away from the air holes and off the treacherous ice and keep them as sheltered as possible while at the same time making the best use of the browse—the only nourishment left.

He thought of the railroad where, once the track was plowed clear again, trains would be running. Eastward lay the farm country of the Middle West, a storehouse of hay and grain. But no man had enough money to bring in such feed in a quantity sufficient to do any good. Economically it would be ruinous, although when a man weighed the question against the suffering of the cattle that fact was lessened in importance. He was tempted to take all the money he had, buy all the feed it would buy, then scatter it to go as far as it would. That was not a sane thought, yet just where a man lost possession of his sanity Benteen could not have said.

They moved forward hour after hour, seeing the drifting cattle on either hand as far as vision could travel. Some were bogged helplessly in the drifts, motionless, perhaps dead on their feet. Others lay stretched on the flats and in the gullies, dead or dying. It seemed almost a painted scene from the brush of an artist either mad or infinitely compassionate.

Around four in the afternoon, with night already coming on, they arrived upon the breaks above the river valley. Benteen, chilled beyond feeling, sat his saddle, staring down.

The bottom swarmed with cattle. Shannon, whose course they had followed all the way, had moved continually down the wind from Sage and Bitter creeks. The right- and left-hand reaches, of perhaps a dozen miles of the bottom, would confine almost all the drift from that region. Benteen saw riders at work down there, plunging their horses through the heavy snowpack; and he saw a surprisingly large number of cattle on the river ice.

Suddenly Kinder cursed savagely and pointed a mittened hand.

"Look—down there!"

Two riders, black specks on the vast ground of white, were shoving a staggering little cut of steers toward the frozen river. They hazed and heckled the numbed creatures, driving them relentlessly, forcing them onto the ice.

Friday exploded. "They're not pushin' their own stuff out there, you bet! Nick, Shannon's trying to hold the bottom for his Slash S steers!"

Benteen had already gathered that in sick, disbelieving shock. Some of the steers managed to keep upright on the slick ice, others went down to stay. A few of those farther out were making their way to the far bank. He could see a number of cattle over there, drifting dumbly on toward the snow-blanketed prairie.

Then he realized there were men working on that side, also, making sure the unwanted cattle kept moving.

He saw in an instant what Bitter Creek now faced.

From where he sat he could count a dozen riders, working the cattle on the bottomland. More of the half dead creatures were filtering down through the breaks. A rifle cracked somewhere.

The men watching from the bluff top swept staggered eyes to each other.

"We gonna stop that, boys?" Kinder asked finally.

"Easy," Benteen said, hardly recognizing his voice. "Shannon's gonna fight for that bottom. He's got two-three times that many men spread along the river."

"We gonna stop it?" Kinder repeated.

"We're gonna stop it. You boys wait here. I'm goin' down there."

He rode out at once, fearing he would be unable to stop the others from a head-on rush into the bottom. Shannon knew that his plans for keeping Bitter Creek stuff out of the valley—or sending it out onto the ice—would be opposed violently. He would be prepared, and Benteen had no intention of letting his men drive into the man's own setup.

He found a place where he could get down. At the bottom of the short, sharp descent, dragged by cow tracks, he saw carcasses. The animals had been shot down. This was no longer a surprise to him, but a couple of the brands he saw were shocking. The Quarter Moon and N Bar—both Sage Creek irons.

Shannon's turned on his neighbors, even, Benteen thought. *He's out to save Slash S now and the hell with everybody else.*

Benteen rode no farther. Shannon's own survival plan—wholly heartless—was now completely clear. With his early start he had been able to spend two days shooting the drifting steers that bore a brand other than his own, and before long he would have the descents from the wind-torn, killing bluff tops choked with carcasses.

Meanwhile he was cutting out the alien brands already on the bottom and crowding them onto the ice to perish, with the few that managed to get across being pushed on south. It would take a terrific fight to stop him.

Benteen retraced his own course. The waiting men watched his quick return with wondering eyes. He told them about the dead Quarter Moon and N Bar steers, dropped by Slash S bullets.

"In the pinch he turned his back on men who've supported him straight down the line?" Dennis asked incredulously.

"He don't figure they'll be in business after this winter, anyhow," Friday reflected. "While he will if he can."

Faced by the enormity of the thing, Benteen's men were ready to wait for the nesters to reach the river. Even then they would be a pitifully small force against the one Shannon had organized so carefully. They pulled back to a coulee they had passed and there waited.

The oil-soaked pine splinters the men had learned to carry helped them get a sage fire started against a coulee bluff that broke the driving force of the wind. Night closed in, but the fire attracted the men with the cavvy and sleigh. They were soon camped.

The nesters received the news of what had been found here at the river with dull apathy. Viciousness and self-serving came out of Shannon as naturally as his own sweat. It had worn them until it seemed, at last, that there was no way to turn. Except for the nighthawk, they bedded down.

Benteen awakened in a bitter dawn. The air was still clear of snow when he looked out from under his soogans, but it had not warmed a degree. It was a goading irony to remember that should the wind shift farther to the west it might yet save the range. The chinook. But that couldn't happen yet, certainly not in time.

He rose quietly, pulled on his boots and wrappings, then freshened the fire that had been kept burning through the night. He poured hot coffee into a cup, waited to let the rim of the metal warm, then drank it. He warmed the bit of his horse's bridle, saddled and rode out without arousing anybody else.

Day was by then only a pale light across the eastern skyline. His feet, encased in their ice-coated boots, were still comfortable but hurt a little, tender from the many times they had been turned into feelingless lumps. His eyes stung and his head ached from their unrelieved recording of the unchanging white.

Inwardly he was feeling an anger such as he had not felt in his life. It was entirely personal now, directed solely against the man who had seized for his own salvation the bottom of the protective valley. He had not forgotten his decision to kill Shannon before the last blizzard had struck. It was firm in him now. He was going down there and have it out.

He had determined the day before that there were only two negotiable drops from the benchland in the immediate vicinity, probably not many more up and down the line. He chose the same one he had used the day before when he started down, riding up on it slowly.

He knew that each of them was being watched closely so that unwanted cattle could be prevented from coming down. He dismounted while still cut from sight from below and moved forward on foot, coming down into the notch broken on the cliff-face, sliding a little from the pitch in the snow.

He passed half a dozen carcasses dropped by bullets along the descent, again observing beyond question that two of them wore Sage Creek brands other than Slash S. He moved on down a few paces, very wary because of the snow-plastered brush and rock immediately at the bottom of the bluffs.

A rifle cracked, a bullet tore between his left arm and side. It ripped through the cloth of the sleeve, jerking the arm back. Benteen was at once flat in the snow against the side of the notch, his gun in his hand. He did not shoot, not yet.

Nor did the man guarding this descent. Benteen's gaze swept hungrily over the ground below, seeking telltale boot tracks or hovering smoke from the gun. There were too many tracks, and the wind had already torn away the smoke. The man was well concealed, and Benteen knew that trying to go farther down would be stupid. He began to slither backward, shocked suddenly to see that he was smearing a little redness on the snow. He couldn't feel it, could use the arm, but it had been cut by that bullet.

When he got back on top and out of sight from the bottom, Benteen rose to his feet. His sleeve was soaking with blood. He mounted and headed back to the camp, which was too far off for the sound of the shot to have carried. But when he rode in, men were stirring, eating breakfast.

Wad Dennis saw the stained coat sleeve and said, "By God—somebody winged you!"

Dismounting, Benteen stepped in behind the windbreak and pulled off his two coats. The bitter air cut through him. He unbuttoned the cuff and pushed up the soggy sleeve. Blood was running down his arm. The flesh on the inside of the upper arm had been slashed. It was at a level where, if the bullet had gone five inches to the right, it would have smashed into his heart.

Fadiman was already bringing heated snow water in the wash pan.

"They saw us yesterday," Benteen said. "And Shannon decided to kill all foreigners tryin' to get down there—beast or man. He's gonna get that bottom worked clean of everything but his own steers. And only needs another day or two to cut it. The main part of the drift come down with the last storm. He figures he's got all the bottom can carry down there already and that it'll be enough to get him started in business again."

"We got to get down there," Fadiman said. "That's all."

"It won't be the way I tried to. He'd plug them descents with human bodies instead of steers. It wouldn't make much difference to him, the state he's in."

CHAPTER NINETEEN

HIS WOUND DRESSED, his two heavy coats back on again, Benteen hunkered at the fire with a cup of coffee, the only breakfast he felt like eating. Con Shannon had stepped completely outside the law in this illegal seizure. One recourse would be to go to Yellow Bluff, wire for Jess Wilson and get the sheriff up here on the next train. He could swear in deputies in sufficient force to take the valley away from Shannon and his big gun crew.

But before that could be accomplished the cattle Shannon was throwing out of the valley would be dead on the river ice or in the drifts on south. The rest would have died on top the bluffs.

Taking Wad Dennis with him, Benteen moved back to the bluff top, picking a point between the descents so as not to attract attention immediately. Staring out across the valley, his arm beginning to hurt, Benteen could see the men starting to work the cattle down there the same as the day before.

Wad's eyes had strayed downstream toward Yellow Bluff, cut from sight by the distance.

"That looks like a snow plow comin' through," he said suddenly.

Benteen swung his own attention in the same direction. The snow completely obliterated the railroad tracks on the far side of the river, their presence being indicated only by the line of telegraph poles. But far down he could see a heavy plume of smoke rising into the frigid overhead, and the two fanning wings of thrown snow that the plow hurled out.

They sat there for some time watching the heavy equipment come closer. Then they swung their horses right, riding on west, keeping themselves as inconspicuous as possible but watching the bottom. They had gone some distance when, at the upper edge of a grove of trees, Benteen saw smoke across the river.

"There's their camp," he said. "Such as it is. Shannon come down without a outfit to make time. Must be dependin' on what they can pack up the tracks from Yellow Bluff. If we had time, we could starve 'em out, maybe. But our own steers wouldn't last that long. They got to mount a clock-around guard now. Must be some men sleepin' there at the camp right now."

"What you thinkin'?"

"How I wish I could get down there and shoot it up."

"Try a feather in each ear and another—"

"I'll wait till I'm dead to start flyin'."

The snow plow was coming on more swiftly than Benteen would have thought possible, throwing up its high banks on either side of the track. That at least was going to form a fence to keep the cattle that managed to cross the ice from going south of the right-of-way. He and Wad waited there as the big rig growled and tore its way abreast of them, then moved on west.

Something was following it that now centered Benteen's interest. Four men were pumping a handcar that drew behind it one of the little flats that section hands used to carry tools to the job. The flat was piled with some kind of freight. It kept on behind the plow until it was abreast the Shannon camp, then stopped. The pumpers got down and began to carry the freight in to the camp, which must have been set up over there for that purpose.

A slow excitement stirred in Benteen; at first he didn't know just why. He said, "Shannon's got a big outfit to feed, and they probably been goin' pretty lean. Wad, we're ridin' down to Yellow Bluff."

"What for?"

"I've got a hunch worth actin' on."

They stopped by the Bitter Creek camp to tell the others where they were going. Fadiman wanted to accompany them. The three put their horses east along the wind-punished bluff top until an hour later they came to the Yellow Bluff road. The ferry was tied up, locked in by the freeze, but dirt had been scattered on the ice to make it easy to cross. They came into a town whose streets were choked with snow shoveled off of roofs and sidewalks.

They left their horses at the end of the street and took to the sidewalk. "We've earned us a drink," Wad said as they came abreast the Longhorn saloon, and Benteen agreed with that. They turned in.

The place was fuller than he would have expected, Benteen noted as he stepped up to the bar with Wad and Fadiman. They were probably unemployed punchers Shannon had not wanted or who had refused to throw in with him. But they looked unduly interested in the new arrivals, Benteen thought. Then Fadiman poked him in the side.

"Larch and Butler back there," the nester whispered. "Sage Basiners you seen on the roundup—remember?"

Benteen took a casual look in the direction Fadiman indicated, but the inspection he made was closer than before. Fadiman was right, and now he remembered some of the punchers sitting about, all more or less disguised by their bundled appearance. They might still be his enemies, but he wondered if they knew they were no longer Shannon's allies.

There was one way to find out. He tossed off his drink, turned and walked down to the table where Larch and Butler sat. They looked morose, yet they watched him suspiciously.

"Howdy," Benteen said. "How come you're not out

with your old playmate?"

Butler was a florid man, almost lost in the heavy clothing he wore even indoors. Truculently, he said, "What's that to you?"

"Plenty. Shannon's shootin' our steers, the same as yours, and hazin' the rest onto the ice. You know that, don't you?"

"Yeah," Butler said. "We know it." Anger deepened the red of his cheeks.

"We need each other, men," Benteen said quietly. "How come you found out about it?"

Butler threw back a questioning look, less angry suddenly. His eyes met Larch's; they glanced back at Benteen. "Shannon hired one of the hands I laid off last fall," he said, still seeming uncertain. "But the man wouldn't go along with it when he found out what Shannon aimed to do. He slipped off and come up to warn us." Temper burst through the restraints then. "That schemin' Shannon told us to stay home—he'd look out for our stuff down here! Just wantin' to keep us out of the way till he'd cut our throats!"

"How many men did you bring?" Benteen asked.

"All we kept on for the winter. Half a dozen between us. Which ain't nearly enough. None of these town people have got the nerve to go out there and help us deal with Shannon. The son of a gun picked the toughest customers he could hire."

"I got a dozen men."

"He's got three dozen. Brung a big crew down here then doubled it."

"They're scattered out," Benteen said.

"But watchful as rattlesnakes."

Benteen hooked a chair rung with his toe, swung the chair out and seated himself. He spoke in a voice lowered so that only the other two men at the table could hear him.

"I ought to laugh at you. But I'm damned if I can laugh at your cattle. We got to root Shannon out of there and be quick about it. I had an idea when I come down here from our camp, and I could use all the help you can give."

"What's the idea?" Larch asked.

"Handcar went up with supplies for Shannon's camp, right behind the snow plow. If I was Shannon I'd buy some oats, too. They didn't bring any cavvy, and what horses they have are working damned hard."

"Let's find out if he's ordered any," Butler said and shoved to his feet.

Telling Wad and Fadiman to wait there, Benteen left with the two ranchers from Sage Basin. They stopped at the general mercantile to discover that the one delivery of groceries was all that was to be made at present. Benteen had expected that, but he learned the identity of the men who had run the handcar. They were townsmen the merchant had hired for the job.

When they reached the feed store, Benteen learned what he wanted to know. Shannon had an order in for oats, a big one. The feed man would start delivering it as soon as the handcar got back.

A brittle light in his eyes, Benteen said, "Man, you're gonna pick sides right now. You must of heard what Shannon's doin'."

"I heard. But who's to stop him? If I refused to deliver that grain, I'd get the hell whaled outta me by some of his toughs."

"It's gonna be delivered, but you aren't gonna do it. All we want from you is a tight mouth. Hear me?"

The man's return stare was unflinching. "If there's any way to turpentine that mad dog, I'm for it."

The plan was quickly finished in a back room at the Longhorn, chosen for privacy. Fadiman and Dennis sat in, the nester still a little suspicious of the men from Sage Basin. But Benteen was convinced that mutual need had brought them together, at least temporarily.

Fadiman would return to the camp and get the men there placed quietly at the descents from the bluff top to the bottom. But they would lie quietly until action started at the camp across the river. Meanwhile Benteen, Dennis, Butler and Larch would take a handcar load of grain to the Shannon camp. The oats would be piled on either side of the little flat car with as many of the Sage Basin punchers as could be accommodated lying between.

"We'll try and take the camp by surprise," Benteen explained, "and grab the horses there. When we start the shootin' Eph's men will try to come down the descents. It's got to be fast and it's got to click, for a good half of Shannon's men are out workin' the cattle. We'll soon have 'em on top of us."

Fadiman looked at Butler, remembering many things out of the past. "How do you know we won't throw you out, ourselves, if we manage to take over the bottom? We got the most men. And we're outlaws."

Butler's face slackened. Then he shook his head. "I reckon we showed some mighty bad judgment, Eph. More ways than one."

"Then let's get at it," said Fadiman, relishing his triumph.

He headed back for the nester camp at once. A little later the handcar came pumping back from the Shannon camp, pulling its empty little dolly. The Sage Basiners put themselves at Benteen's disposal, and to Wad, Benteen said, "You mosey around town and stop anybody you see that looks like he might sneak off to warn Shannon."

A team and sled pounded its way to the railroad tracks where the dolly and handcar waited. When the two rows of grain sacks were built up on the sides of the flat, there was room for four men to lie end to end between, making a total of eight in the party that would try to seize the camp. Wad was one of them, a man Benteen always wanted along when he could get him. They started up the track at once, himself and Dennis pumping across the teetering bars from Butler and Larch.

The load was heavy, the track slick, and it was slow,

hard work. By the time they had moved half a mile up-river from Yellow Bluff, Benteen was warm for the first time since he had left Bar D.

They made progress steadily. The town fell behind, the bottoms on either hand cut off by the snowbanks left by the plow. They seemed to labor in an eye-blinding, elongated world in which the only contrast was themselves and the two black lines of the rails.

They knew they were abreast the Shannon camp only when they saw the tramped snow left by the former handcar operators and the torn place on the north snowbank where the men had climbed over and back moving the stores. The handcar came to a stop, and the men rested a moment, breathing heavily. The four men who had stretched out got up, stiff and cold.

"All right," Benteen said finally. "We go in with a sack of oats on our shoulders. Guns holstered but ready to grab. Just follow my lead."

Grim men nodded.

Heaving up a sack of grain, Benteen balanced it on his shoulder. Since it would be unwise to move in heavily armed, the weapons were all under coats. But bottom buttons had been left unfastened. Under his load, he staggered up the snowbank to the top. The camp was about five hundred feet ahead. He saw a man cooking at the fire, a couple of others sitting about, knew more were sleeping from the previous night's guard duty. He saw about a dozen horses on picket close to the camp. He stumbled down the other side of the snowbank, following the tracks already tramped from there to the camp.

The men at the camp were watching. Even the horses swung their heads with interest, as if sensing the feed coming up. He waited for the men to show some sign of alarm when they observed how many men were moving in. His mouth tightened at the corners. It had been too much to hope that Shannon could be caught here.

He was within a hundred feet of the camp when a man there shoved to a hasty stand, staring hard. He said something that caused everyone else to move energetically.

Benteen put his oat sack down slowly, as if pausing to rest. He let it fall flat. But all of them ahead were bolting for the cover of the heaped-up camp supplies. He saw some men come out of their blankets, scrambling. Benteen's men ran out on his flanks, dropped their sacks.

"Come outta there!" Benteen shouted forward. "Or we'll blast you out!"

The answer was a sharp crack of a pistol.

Benteen's men went down as one, each behind his grain sack. Remembering the number of descents to be guarded, Benteen judged that there might have been half a dozen men asleep there, although he had been unable to count them. A couple more shots were let go over there, hasty and aimless.

The sacks of grain now came in for an even more important use. Benteen and his men began to roll and push them ahead, fanning out so as to move in on either side of the camp as much as possible. They worked slowly, stubbornly, keeping themselves protected by the sacks, not yet ready to return fire. By then Benteen was aware of shooting up on the bluffs across the river. Fadiman's men were trying to drive down. They would be hung up awhile at best.

When he was out far enough to angle his shots in to the camp, Benteen stopped bellying forward and pushing the cumbersome sack. Wad was off on his left, Butler and the others farther yet, curving a little about the pile of stores. Benteen sent a bullet whistling low to the snow, across the camp. He saw empty soogans that men had left hastily to get in behind the stores. His shot was answered with a fusillade.

His jaw clamped hard. In a few moments men were going to pull in on horses from their scattered places on the bottom. He had to move farther forward so there would be no cover left around the heap of stores. But he could not shove his protecting sacked oats sideways from a flattened position, and to skew it around so it would roll would be to expose himself to the waiting Slash S outfit.

Every few seconds men on both sides let go with an impatient bullet that either hammered into the stores or sped harmlessly across the snow. Leaving his grain sack where it lay, Benteen began to slide himself backward. When he had retreated a considerable distance, he began to inch forward. The cold of the snow seemed to have reduced his flesh to its own temperature, but there was worry in his feeling, too, for he was exposed broadside to the camp should a Slash S man happen to notice him.

Then all at once he found what he had hoped for, the trough dug by a horse moving in to the camp. He rolled into it and for a moment lay breathing heavily, hearing the shooting on the far rim as well as here. He could move faster when he started again, the packed groove he followed hiding and protecting him.

He was almost up to the picketed horses when he stopped. He took the time to replace the spent cartridges in his .45. He unfastened the cloth battening down his hat, removed the hat and placed it beside him. Then he began to lift his head until his eyes were on a level with the top of the groove, not knowing when the thread of his life would be snapped.

He drew no fire.

Lifting himself a little higher, he ran his eyes over the exposed back side of the store pile. He could see the flattened shapes of men; a few were hunkered, protected yet ready to act at the first chance.

"Drop them guns," he yelled.

The men on their feet whipped around, shooting. Benteen lay there, his own piece hot in his hand. For a moment he was all alone against them while Wad and the others took in the meaning of the movement he had made. Realizing the Sage Basiners were distracted from the rear, Wad and the others dropped caution. They kicked snow as they shoved themselves around into place and joined in.

Benteen had flattened all the Slash S riders by then and he knew some of them had dropped from his bullets. Then he had to drop down into his protection as his smoking gun clicked empty. He was grateful for the quick support of his comrades, whose bitter gun chatter kept the enemy pinned down while he reloaded, his fingers trembling in their repressed excitement.

By the time he had finished shoving in fresh loads, one phase of the fight was over.

"All right, for God's sake!" a man yelled. "We quit!"

"Get up on your hind legs," Wad called out.

Peering carefully, Benteen saw four men climb to a stand, their arms pointed upward. He rose slowly, ready to fire should somebody on the ground prove less helpless than indicated. But the four men upright would not have exposed themselves to so many covering guns had it been a trick. He moved in.

Three men lay dead on the snow, three more were wounded and helpless.

"Take their guns while I cover 'em," Benteen said to Wad. "I don't care what they do afterward. Butler, the rest of you better throw saddles on some horses. Help if we can get Fadiman's outfit joined up with us before we have to meet the rest of Shannon's."

It was done quickly. Wad gathered the Slash S firearms and dropped them into a nosebag which he carried on the crook of his arm when he and Benteen plunged out to where the others were hastily saddling horses. Benteen rose to leather and from that elevated view saw horsemen forming into a group up the valley, on the other side of the river.

Shannon's men, in their work, were scattered out for miles. Some of them would not even be aware of the fighting as yet. Benteen had counted on that, wanted to get this step in the action over before Shannon could get organized. His saddle mates, all intact, moved their new horses against the snow, heading toward the river. With it quiet here, Benteen could make out the continued shooting at the bluffs.

CHAPTER TWENTY

THEY CHOSE THE DESCENT from the bluff tops closest to the Shannon and nester camps and moved in at a rush. Half a dozen Slash S men, thinking the main attack had been launched there in an effort to breach into the valley, had moved in to the defense. Due to his difficult position, Fadiman had been unable to fight his way down. Benteen led his men in from the rear. Like those at the camp previously, the Shannon men forted at the foot of the drop-down let them get in close before they realized something was wrong.

Benteen threw himself and his seven men into a short, hot fight, then the three Slash S hirelings still alive threw up their hands. Bought loyalty was not enough to cause them to die at their posts. Shannon had never commanded any other kind.

Benteen rode on to the top and joined Fadiman. He sent the other nesters upstream and down to the remaining gaps. There was no use in their fighting their way down at those points now, and he told them to concentrate here where a bridgehead had been established on the bottom. He and Fadiman sat their horses at the cliff's edge, studying the situation below them.

Shannon's men had been scattered up and down and across the river. The party Benteen had noticed previously was waiting for others to join it. Now he could see another and smaller party off in the other direction. He wished he knew which one Shannon was with.

"Anyhow, we whittled 'em down a little closer to our

size," Fadiman commented. "And so far we ain't lost a man."

"We've hardly got started, Eph," Benteen warned. "I wish them two outfits'd come together."

"Shannon can't be with both. And the other's not sure what to do."

Benteen was already shaping his next move. He waited with Fadiman where he was until the other nesters had come in. He then had twenty-one men brought together, but estimated that the force remaining to Shannon was still much larger. He divided his own outfit into three parties, two of which he scattered out along the bluff top at its edge, on either side of the descent. Some of them had rifles and carbines.

He had his Texans in his own group, plus Fadiman and Damon. "We'll round in a cut of steers up here," he said, "and start it down. That'll bring Shannon's gunhawks in fast. You boys on top play dead till they get in close enough so you can cut 'em up. Let's get moving."

All along the wind-harried bluff top, steers stood waiting to drop dead. A few had to be a sacrifice for the rest, and Benteen's riders began to haze the strongest together. When they had thus made up a cut of around fifty head, Benteen signaled that it would be enough.

He said quietly, "Want to ride point with me, Wad?"

"Can't say I want to," Wad answered. "But I'm goin' to."

They got the exhausted animals moving slowly. A signal from Butler at the rim told Benteen to proceed, that Shannon's men were still holding off. There was a tightness in his chest, and he wondered if Shannon would strike at the bait. It was probable he would be misled into thinking a much larger gather of cattle had been made on top, that the attack on the camp had been undertaken to clear the way for it to start down. Shannon would have to stop that, but he was a sly man and might see through the strategy.

Benteen dropped into the notch ahead of the weak-

ened steers, Wad immediately following him. They
came out through the lower rubble and brush, where
it became apparent that the two parties standing off in
the distance were still motionless. But not for long. The
first steers came into view on the flat. The party to the
west started moving. A moment later the one downstream did likewise. They were all pushing their horses.
Benteen had a cold smile on his lips, knowing they
were seeing a thousand steers pour out of the notch.

Kinder and Friday came out of the descent, then the
others, but none of them emerged from the concealing
brush at the bottom. The western outfit of Slash S
riders was the larger and closer. Since it had moved first
Benteen figured that Shannon was with it, giving the
order.

He and Wad pulled out presently, letting the steers
file slowly between them. Then the crackle of shooting
came through the cold air to them. Benteen swung his
horse and fired toward the big bunch coming from the
west. One of them had a rifle, and in a moment a steer
went down.

Benteen and Wad kept shooting as the oncomers
hammered their way closer, getting in range. Then they
fell back toward the gap, none of the men there or on
top having yet pitched into the fight. But Shannon's
men were firing enough to keep the atmosphere deafen-
ing. More steers went down. Benteen and Dennis forted
up with their comrades at the bottom of the descent.

Shannon's men made short work of the steers that had
invaded what they called their own territory, then
swung toward the notch to destroy the foothold gained
by their enemies, the parties united now, their blood
hot from the smell of powder smoke. Only Benteen and
the men on the bottom with him retaliated, those on
top of the bluff remaining quiet.

But the present return fire was heated enough to
make the Slash S outfit fling out of saddle and burrow
into the snow. The excited riderless horses wheeled
back. So far it was working out the way Benteen had

figured it might, and Slash S was pinned down. With his men he began to make a slow withdrawal up the notch. The enemy crowded in closer.

Then the guns on top joined in.

Belatedly Con Shannon realized he had let his wild possessiveness of the valley and the excitement of his men carry them into a trap. Benteen recognized his voice, almost a scream: "Dig in. Hold steady!"

It was bad advice, for the men on top of the cliff had elevation to angle their bullets in sharply. Yet the enemy had no real alternative but to dig in to the snow. For a moment the shooting was one-sided, while men worked like moles, clawing down into some kind of protection from the hail of searching lead. Some of them died or were knocked out of it in that interval. Yells, sharp and helpless, cut into the dispute of the guns.

It settled into a deadly give and take but remained one-sided. Where moments before Shannon had possessed superiority, he was now outthought, outfought, and his hold on the valley he coveted was beginning to break. His men were suffering the damage, the others were well protected. If Shannon didn't realize it all, his hirelings did. But they had to fight for their lives, and this generated its own, personalized fury.

The end was signaled when a man on top yelled urgently.

"Benteen—somebody's managed to pull out! I think it's Shannon! To the right! He got hold of a horse!"

The voice was Butler's, and it bewildered Benteen. Shannon could have dug his way carefully through the snow, when he realized the fight was lost, and got into the brush, then moved down and managed to catch one of the loose horses. Yet Butler could be using a clever trick to take the heart out of the man's fighters.

Benteen knew it was the truth when the voice of Shannon made no denial.

Whatever panic was thrown into Shannon's men by the same realization, they had not surrendered, might prefer to fight it to a finish. Benteen wanted Shannon, as he had never wanted to face another man in all his life. He began to work his way back up the notch. Soon he had enough cover and could rise to a stand and was speedily on top.

He could see the rider, then, making for the railroad tracks and its better underfooting.

Benteen swung toward the closest horse, went up to the saddle. He rode back to the rim, needing to see whether Shannon turned east or west along the plowed railroad. Direct pursuit was out of the question, Benteen knew, for by the time he could get down one of the other descents and across the space to the tracks, Shannon would be too far ahead.

Shannon topped over the near snowbank along the right-of-way. From his elevation Benteen could see the man turn east, toward Yellow Bluff. Shannon was thinking in desperate shrewdness now, knowing that a bullet might be a kindly death to the one deserved for what he had done to his friends as well as his enemies. He wanted a fresh horse under him, blankets, food, was heading for Yellow Bluff to get them.

Benteen hesitated only a moment, then turned his horse east along the bluff top, following the route he had ridden with Fadiman only that morning. He rode in a sick dread that Shannon would manage to elude him, crowded his horse for all it could give without wasting it heedlessly. It seemed an hour before he reached the road from Bitter Creek to the town. He was soon across the river.

He knew he could not possibly have beaten Shannon to the place. He came onto the snow-heaped main street cautiously. Then he saw a spent, heaving Slash S horse outside the livery stable. The man was inside, getting another mount, perhaps at gun point. Benteen dismounted where he was and left his own horse.

Thus he was planted on the shoveled sidewalk when, a moment later, Con Shannon came out the livery door leading a horse. Shannon looked the other way first,

toward the railroad tracks along which he expected to
be followed. Then his head swung and he saw Benteen.

"Waited a long while for this, Shannon," Benteen
called. "You got a choice yet. Hang—or fill your hand."

The frozen look evaporated from Shannon as he drew
and shot. The bullet dug up splinters between Benteen's spread feet. Maybe Shannon lived to hear the
crash of the gun that killed him, although the bullet
traveled faster. When he dropped there was a hole
above his right eye.

·Benteen left him there. He took the fresh livery horse,
swung to saddle and headed for the railroad tracks.

The fight on the bottom was over. The Texans, nesters and Sage Basiners who were still on their feet had
rounded up a dozen prisoners, located that many more
wounded, while the rest of those who had cared to join
Shannon's cause had paid the supreme penalty. Yet the
victory had not been without cost. In the last, furious
fight Burt Friday and two of the Sage Basin punchers
had been killed. Fadiman had been shot through the
thick of the thigh, but nobody knew about it until
afterward. Wad Dennis had lost a finger.

Butler looked long at Benteen before he spoke.

"Don't know how to say this, man. But you've won
your place in this country, and so's your Bitter Creek
neighbors. Sage Basin's behind you from here on."

"That says it," Benteen answered. It was still hard
traveling, that March day, when he and his men rode
back to Bitter Creek. The warm wind had come at last,
the chinook, and started its thawing. Water already
flooded the gullies, the tracks in the road, the dwindling
snow was heavy and soggy. This mass swallowed the
carcasses that Benteen knew neither he nor any other
cattleman would be eager to count. The loss had been
terrific, but not complete. The range would come back
stronger than before. He knew it already, even though
there hadn't as yet been a steer on the Yellowstone
strong enough to drive home.

At the Meadows's side road, Wad Dennis slowed his

horse. "I reckon I'll turn in here, boys," he said.

Benteen smiled at him. "Luck, Wad."

"Mebbe it's a little early to speak to her, but I reckon she needs me."

"And knows it," Benteen agreed.

The others peeled off one by one, and Benteen rode on toward Bar D with his Texans. That was wrong, he reflected. They were Montanans now. A part of it, no longer outlaws. The six hopeless weeks they had ridden the river with the other outfits had proved that, even while they all watched their herds dwindle to the point of vanishing.

He was glad Wad felt as he did about Edith Meadows, and he was remembering, also, how Kit had come to him a month ago, recovered from his wound, to tell him beforehand that Cassie was in Yellow Bluff, that they hoped to be married there.

Now they were coming over the last rise before dropping down to Bar D headquarters. It wasn't a big outfit, but he knew that with the right range management it and all the other spreads on Bitter Creek could again be big enough. Acres would count less when men knew how to use them, and this winter had taught them many things.

He smiled when he saw Linda had splashed right out into the slush of the yard, up to her knees, to watch him come in with his men.

He swung out of the saddle beside her, and his Montana cowhands, smiling, had the good sense to move on.